Who is the book For?

"Non Verbal" is a poignant and illuminating narrative crafted for a diverse audience. It speaks directly to parents who are navigating the challenging journey of raising a child with developmental disabilities, offering them solace, empathy, and valuable insights. Additionally, educators, healthcare professionals, and caregivers will find immense value in its pages, gaining a deeper understanding of the complexities involved in supporting individuals with developmental disabilities. Moreover, this book serves as a beacon of awareness for society at large, fostering empathy and compassion towards those living with disabilities. Ultimately, "Non Verbal" is a compelling testament to the resilience of the human spirit and a powerful call to embrace diversity and inclusion in all facets of life.

CONTENTS

NON VERBAL

Author

Shannon Elaine Williams

Non Verbal

Chapter 1: Labor Begins

A crisp breeze swept through the neighborhood, causing the leaves of Oak trees to cascade gracefully to the ground, painted in hues of autumn. The wind carried with it the melodies of nature, a whispered tune only the dancing leaves seemed to hear. Late September marked the transition of seasons, with the once humid 90-degree days giving way to refreshing winds that accompanied the night.

A car quietly traversed the serene street, passing by charming bungalow houses, each with its unique sense of majesty. The occupants of the car stole a glance at a well-manicured brick home, its facade, a blend of brown brick and wood, hinting at a construction date back in the '60s. A partially open curtain in the front window offered a glimpse into the intimate details of the home, briefly revealing one of its owners as they moved about. This was the dwelling of Marcus and Layla Evans, a couple bound by years of marriage and the anticipation of their first child, a precious hope rising from the shadows of four miscarriages.

Marcus, tall, with a smooth dark complexion was very handsome and masculine. Sipping a cup of coffee, his expression bore a blend of contentment and meditation. As he squinted at the hot liquid, one couldn't help but wonder if the coffee required more than the generous three cups of sugar he had just added. Placing the cup down, he turned his head, reaching for a napkin to tidy up after indulging in a muffin.

"Bae?" he called out to Layla, finding her in the Master Bedroom grappling with the challenge of putting on her shoes. Concern laced his voice, "You okay?" Layla, exhibiting the familiar signs of the pains of pregnancy, released a sigh and adjusted herself on the bed before responding.

"Yeah, I'm okay... (whew) baby's kicking again," she assured, slowly rising with evident swelling from face to ankles. Her maternity gown barely contained the protruding belly as she felt for the baby's movements. Another kick elicited a subtle expression of discomfort, prompting Layla to speak softly and unintelligibly, perhaps in a silent conversation with the divine to ease the challenges of pregnancy.

Both Layla and Marcus, hailing from the Bible belt, were devoted Sunday morning churchgoers who sought to integrate Christian teachings into their daily lives. Nightly prayers became a ritual, entwined with pleas for guidance, financial stability, health, and spiritual well-being. With Layla's pregnancy, their prayers intensified, revolving around the health of their unborn child. The common fears of expecting parents, regarding potential complications or more severe scenarios, stirred a heightened anxiety, an emotion palpable in the couple's every prayer and shared concern.

Layla maneuvers down the hallway with utmost care, one hand on her stomach and the other seeking support from the wall. Another sigh escapes her lips, and she closes her eyes momentarily, concentrating on each deliberate step. When she opens her eyes, her husband stands at the end of the hall, his expression reflecting concern for her evident discomfort. The pain she endures is unmistakable, evident in her slow and laborious movement.

"Come on, I got you," he murmurs softly, making his way toward her. Gently, he places his arm around her shoulders, guiding her up the hallway. She perspires lightly, a clear sign that the labor pains are taking a toll, perhaps even affecting her blood pressure. "You're soaked. We have to get you to the hospital. Pain coming more?" he asks with empathy as they approach the front door. Another kick from the baby prompts a wince, further confirming her distress. "How far apart?" he inquires. Her eyes convey the answer, affirming his concerns for her condition.

"About every five or six minutes, I guess," she manages to say amidst the laborious effort. He nods sympathetically and opens the door for her. The sun dips below the horizon, and a brisk wind persists. Layla welcomes the cool air, despite the shivers caused by her perspiration. Marcus, attuned to her needs, attempts to shield her from the cold before they make their way to the car. Autumn leaves swirl in a gust of wind, settling gently onto the lawn. Marcus secures his wife into the car with meticulous care, ensuring her safety and that of their unborn child before walking around to the driver's side.

Chapter 2: Heading to the Hospital

Traffic buzzes on the busy avenue in front of the towering Luke Memorial Hospital. People in smocks or scrubs briskly move between the parking lot and the hospital entrance. Some are engrossed in conversations on cell phones or engrossed in paperwork, while others, possibly patients or their visitors, navigate with varying levels of urgency.

Into this hustle, a gray sedan, driven by Marcus with his pregnant wife Layla, enters the parking lot. Layla's pain is now more evident, with perspiration and quick pants of air signaling her distress. Marcus, concerned, places a loving hand on hers to provide comfort.

"We're here now, bae. Just relax," Marcus reassures her. Layla nods with closed eyes, continuing to release short pants. After navigating the congested parking lot, Marcus spots an SUV vacating a space conveniently near the Emergency entrance. Layla, noticing the available spot, silently offers a prayer of gratitude.

Nurses briskly traverse the corridor in front of the electronic doors, each headed to their designated areas. The hum of life-preserving electronic equipment echoes through the Emergency room foyer, while the sharp scent of disinfectants fills the air. Coughs from those seeking medical attention create a backdrop to the low murmur of patients and nursing assistants exchanging information.

As an elderly man with an aluminum walker approaches the electronic doors, they smoothly open, revealing Marcus accompanying his wife. Her breathing becomes labored, and she clutches her stomach, unmistakably in pain. Marcus assists her, signaling the imminent onset of labor. A young Caucasian male nurse notices the couple and approaches to offer assistance.

"Hi, um... is she going into labor?" the young nurse inquires, reaching for Layla's hand. Marcus nods affirmatively, prompting the nurse to turn towards the reception desk. The African American nurses assistant behind the desk, engaged in a phone call regarding a patient with diabetes, quickly relays the information and rises to her feet, motioning for the nurse to guide the couple toward the double doors.

"Set her in this wheelchair," the receptionist instructs. The male nurse's assistant complies, assisting Marcus in easing Layla into the wheelchair. Concern etches Marcus's face as the receptionist inquires about Layla's contractions, adjusting the wheelchair stoppers. Layla, her discomfort evident, struggles to breathe. Marcus nods in confirmation, and the double doors open as the male nurse's assistant swiftly wheels her through. The receptionist rushes past to inform a doctor, providing instructions before hurrying back to his desk to answer the phone.

Perspiration glistens on Layla's face as she looks around the corridor and through open doors, the breeze from being pushed along providing a small relief. Yet, the rapidly intensifying pains persist. Grimacing from a kick, she places her hand on her stomach. The male nurse offers comforting assurances as they reach their destination at the end of the hallway. Two smiling nurses greet them, ushering them into a room.

Chapter 3: Emergency Woes

Soon after, the approach of squeaking shoes prompts Marcus to turn towards the footsteps. A doctor, clad in white smocks with pins in the pockets and a stethoscope around his neck, appears. Of Indian or Pakistani descent, he seems to be in his late thirties to early forties.

"Er... how are you? She's having contractions, you say?" the doctor greets, directing his question to Marcus and the nurse's assistant. Other female nurses assist Layla to her feet, preparing to lie her down on a bed. Both Marcus and the nurse's assistant nod in confirmation, with the latter providing additional information and mentioning another medical issue unrelated to Layla's pregnancy. The doctor conveys instructions to the nurse's assistant before turning his attention to Layla as the young man excuses himself. "Er... how far apart are these contractions now?" he inquires further. Layla grimaces as a nurse attaches a blood pressure gauge to her left arm.

"Just relax, baby," the nurse says softly, her compassionate demeanor evident in her warm and comforting, wrinkled eyes. Layla nods, and Marcus responds to the doctor's inquiry, "Oh... about two or three a minutes, I guess." The doctor nods, displaying a hint of concern. He leans over, placing the stethoscope's listening device on Layla's chest. Her chest heaves slightly, eyes closed as she releases short bursts of air. The doctor removes the stethoscope and gestures for Layla to lie flat on the bed. He looks at the two nurses, requesting the electrocardiogram monitor and a device for listening to the unborn baby's heart rate. One nurse swiftly exits the room, and Marcus observes her, noting her red hair and surmising she might be a recent nursing school graduate, possibly around twenty-two or twenty-three years old. His focus returns to his pregnant wife as the older nurse wipes a towel across Layla's head and adjusts the IV unit around the side of the bed.

"Ah... how far along is she in the pregnancy?" the doctor further inquires. Marcus informs him she has just entered into her eighth month. The doctor raises an eyebrow and nods. "I see. Premature birth. Er... is this her first pregnancy?... no... yes? "She's had three miscarriages prior to this pregnancy. So this is her fourth pregnancy." Marcus replies. "Well, everything's going to be ok. Ok?" The doctor reassures with a comforting voice aimed at relaxing and assuring Layla.

"Er... who is her obstetrician?" The doctor continues his inquiries, and Marcus provides the name of Layla's obstetrician.

"Doctor Glyn," he informs, and the doctor nods. "Okay. I will go and inform him of your condition, okay? You will be okay, okay?" The doctor reassures, tucking the clipboard under his arm as he casually walks out of the room, retrieving his cell phone from his pocket. Marcus observes and listens as the doctor communicates with Layla's doctor. Moments later, the ER doctor returns, conveying that Dr. Glyn will be in within the hour, and the nurses will be attending to them. Marcus expresses gratitude, receiving a courteous smile as the doctor exits.

Doctor Dregin, a rather short African American female with beautiful kinky locks, now stands next to Layla as one of the nurses hands her the device for listening to the baby's heartbeat. Layla, still releasing short bursts of air, watches as the doctor retrieves the device. She then instructs the other nurse to begin connecting leads from the vital sign unit to all the monitor pads on Layla's body. Marcus holds Layla's hand, leans forward to kiss her on her head, and whispers something to her. The nurse starts connecting the leads, and the monitor device displays various numbers, graphs, coded sequences, and blips that neither Marcus nor Layla understand. As they watch, the doctor begins rubbing a clear ointment onto Layla's stomach. The other nurse returns with a plastic kit containing medical equipment for administering an IV. Layla, apprehensive about needles, gazes at the kit as the nurse opens it. Recognizing her uneasiness, the other nurse places a comforting hand on Layla's arm, and the doctor continues his preparations.

The doctor retrieves the device designed for listening to the baby's heart and checks the monitor before drawing the couple's attention to it. She explains that as the monitor detects the baby's heartbeat, they will both hear it and see it on the monitor screen. Securing a monitor band around Layla's abdomen, the doctor places the device on her stomach. The nurse's assistants adjust switches and knobs on the monitor unit as Layla and Marcus observe with curiosity. The doctor rubs the device across Layla's stomach, and a low percussion of muffled sound resonates, followed by the rapid beating of the baby's heart. The nurse's assistants marvel at the audible transmission and glance at the screen.

"That's your baby's heart," the older nurse informs them. Despite the pain, Layla stifles a smile, expressing the joy of motherhood. Marcus proudly observes the device and looks up at the monitor screen, showing a grainy image of their baby.

Chapter 4: Learning The Sex

"And there's your baby. Can you see her? It really looks like... yeah, it's a girl alright," the doctor says. The nurses cheer, assuming Layla is overjoyed with the prospect of a daughter. However, Layla's joy stems from the apparent health of the baby, evidenced by the strong heartbeat.

"Is everything okay with the baby?" Layla asks in a strained tone. The doctor, still looking at the screen, explains that the baby has a strong heartbeat and seems well developed for the third trimester. The doctor removes the device, and the nurses begin setting up for more blood work. Layla expresses slight anxiety, having had blood drawn recently. Marcus reassures her, and the nurse assures Layla that it's just another little stick to ensure the well-being of their baby. Layla flinches as the needle enters her skin, and Marcus continues to comfort her during the procedure. Marcus tightens his grip on Layla's hand and softly whispers words of comfort into her ear. As he observes the vial filling with her blood, he finds himself lost in thoughts of their future as a family. Imagining their daughter's milestones, from her first steps to graduation, brings a smile to his lips. They are united in love, and this shared journey enhances the special bond they already have. Marcus places another gentle kiss on Layla's head, but beneath the smile, a hint of uncertainty lingers – a common sentiment for expecting couples. The unpredictability of their child's health, whether mental or physical, shadows his thoughts. The idyllic images of their daughter's future transform into worrisome scenes of medical procedures and whispered diagnoses. Shaking off these negative thoughts, Marcus refocuses just as the nurse withdraws the needle from Layla's arm.

"All done, baby. That wasn't so bad, was it? Nurse Alley, you can go ahead and connect the tubing and get the drip going," the head nurse directs. The other nurses begin connecting the heart monitor to Layla.

"You'll be alright, sweetheart. We're just getting some fluids in you, standard procedure for labor," the older nurse murmurs, gently patting Layla's shoulder. Layla, her fatigue evident and face slightly swollen, nods in understanding. Across the room, Nurse Alley finishes the procedure, and Layla receives a comforting pat on the shoulder from the older nurse. With a smile directed at Marcus, she whispers words of reassurance to them both before quietly leaving the room.

Chapter 5: Anxious Parents

Moments later, nurse Alley, gathering medical supplies, heads toward the door.

"There's a buzzer right next to the bed. If you guys need anything, okay?" she declares, backing out of the room with the rolling table of supplies. Marcus and Layla acknowledge her before watching her exit, her calm demeanor disappearing behind the closing door.

Layla lay still in her bed, her face slightly swollen, with a light perspiration forming a tiny river around her neck. Her breathing was slightly labored, and Marcus observed her having trouble relaxing. Deeply invested in his thoughts, Marcus watched his wife carefully, one hand buried in the lining of his pockets. As he removed his hand to wipe a nervous gesture across his face, he struggled against the demons that had invaded his mind earlier in the day. The discomfort etched on his wife's face made it challenging.

Taking in the room's artwork and medical equipment, Marcus walked over to the vital sign unit. The machine emitted beeps, and various numbers fluctuated, indicating his wife's blood pressure, oxygen level, and most significantly, their baby's heartbeat. The baby's heart rate, now slower than before, alarmed him, intensifying his uncertainty. Just then, a strained voice interrupted his anxious thoughts. Layla had awakened and was staring at him with sullen eyes. Concerned, Marcus looked down at her, alternating his gaze between her and the medical unit before leaning closer.

"Are you okay, babe? You seemed to be having difficulties relaxing...and you're sweating," he said, wiping her forehead. Layla nodded, offering a smile that concealed her discomfort.

"I'm...I'm okay. Just tired. The baby's kicking and moving...oh my God," she stated, running a hand across her forehead. Marcus kissed her, reassuring her that everything would be okay, then glanced at the monitor, listening to the accelerated heartbeat dominating the room's acoustics.

"Her little heart is beating slower than before," Layla whispered, both observing the monitor. Marcus expressed concern, unsure if this was normal.

"I know. That's what concerns me. I don't know...but I guess that's...normal?" he said, confused. Layla smiled.

"She's moving a lot. She seems ready to make her appearance," she stated. While it didn't entirely ease Marcus' mind, hearing the lack of real concern in her voice alleviated some stress. They shared a reflective silence as Marcus pulled a chair closer to her bedside. He squeezed her hand, and despite his lingering anxiety, they remained in quiet companionship.

Layla gazed at Marcus, sensing his tension. She loved him deeply and felt grateful for his caring companionship. Breaking the silence, she softly inquired, "Are you okay?" Marcus, momentarily averting eye contact, responded, "I'm okay, bae. Just thinking about a lot of things." Layla knew it involved their baby. They had discussed the possibilities of defects given the pregnancy's complications and the cesarean.

"It's about the baby, isn't it?" she whispered, withdrawing his hand from hers, nervously rubbing her own hands. Marcus, looking down in shame, nodded in confirmation.

"It's just that...we talked about this...the premature situation. And I was just envisioning her with some type of disability, and...I just..." His words were interrupted as Layla reached for his hand, placing it on her stomach.

"Do you feel that?" she whispered, a smile forming on her face. Marcus stifled a smile as he felt the baby's kick.

"Our little baby girl will be okay," she assured him, providing a moment of reassurance amidst their shared uncertainties.
her. Marcus embraces his wife, showing caution due to the medical equipment. After the embrace, he sits up and looks around the room, expressing concern.

Chapter 6: Nursely Encounter

"I know you're probably hungry, but..." he begins, Layla's expression brightening as she contemplates the dish she'd love to have.

"They don't want me eating anything... but I'd really love to have a big plate of Debbie's pasta with cake and icecream right now," she says, injecting a touch of humor into the conversation, lightening the mood, and eliciting a slight laugh from Marcus.

"You and I both. I'm starving. So... let me go see if I can find something. There's always trays in the little break room," he suggests. Layla nods, attempting to sit up in bed.

"Be still, babe. You're gonna pull out the I.V.," he cautions, rising and heading towards the door. Layla blows out a sigh and grabs her belly.

"Want some of those juice cups?" he asks.

"Ha Ha, funny," she responds, her eyes closing as if doing breathing exercises.

"No. Definitely don't need any more liquid. These fluids have me needing to go to the bathroom right now," she states. Marcus, returning to assist her, removes the covers and observes her swollen ankles. Careful not to disturb those leads, he helps her to her feet. Layla rises slowly, grimacing, and swings her legs over the side of the bed, with Marcus holding her arms. He notices her discomfort and the disarray of her hair.

"Easy, babe," he comforts her as she places her swollen feet on the floor. Her eyes closed, Layla takes her hand to her back, and Marcus maneuvers the I.V. pole for her to hold onto. Slowly walking her to the bathroom door, he feels deep empathy for her condition. Yet, thoughts of their baby girl almost make him smile despite Layla's obvious pain.

"I'll be right back, babe, okay? Will be right down the hallway getting something to eat, okay?" he reassures. Layla nods with her eyes still closed, and he lets the bathroom door close slowly behind her.

In the small snack room nearby, Marcus searches for something to ease his hunger and empathizes with Layla's likely hunger. He releases a sigh, inspects the vending machine's prices, and shakes his head. After retrieving his wallet, he inserts several dollars into the machine, contemplating his choices before finally making a selection. Pushing the button, he watches as a bag of chips drops to the bottom of the machine.
Marcus pushes another button and watches hungrily as the microwavable popcorn falls to the bottom. As he removes his purchase, a young light-skinned RN walks in. She gives a courteous smile as she goes over to a refrigerator, and Marcus returns the warm gesture. He watches as she retrieves some jello cups from the refrigerator and notices many other items within that were

liquid-based. The thought crosses his mind to inquire as to whether or not his wife would be allowed at least to eat these.

"Ah... excuse me..." He calls out to her. The young nurse pauses and turns to his voice. Her expression is still complacent, though her raised eyebrows suggest puzzlement at his approach.

"Oh... the microwave's right here," she states. Seeing that he was holding the popcorn, she assumes that this was his inquiry. Marcus smiles and glances over in the direction of the microwave before looking back at the young woman, and noticing the name on the ID badge.

"Oh, no... I uh... ya see, my wife is in Labor and Delivery and they're expecting that she may have the baby soon. She has to be... extremely hungry. And I was just wondering... I know she can't have solid foods, but could she at least have a couple of those puddings I mean... that's like liquid right?" He implores, almost pleading with the nurse. She smiles and shakes her head to the contrary.

"No. I'm afraid not, sir. If she is in Labor and Delivery, she can't have anything to eat until after the baby is delivered. Sorry." She states in a sympathetic tone of voice. Her voice is very childlike, and Marcus surmises that she is probably fresh from college in her chosen field. She wears no wedding ring, but he surmises that she more than likely has a boyfriend. He wonders whether or not she herself has a child. And if so, is the father in the child's life, or is she doing everything. It isn't uncommon. He nods in understanding, and the nurse turns and walks out of the snack room, her squeaking Nikes echoing as she disappears down the hall. Marcus then turns toward the microwave and opens the door.

As he waits for the popcorn to finish popping, Marcus's thoughts drift back to Layla. He couldn't help but feel a twinge of worry. The situation in the delivery room had been tense, and seeing Layla in discomfort tore at his heart. He hoped fervently for a smooth delivery, with both Layla and the baby coming out healthy. Closing his eyes briefly, he sends out a silent prayer before focusing back on the task at hand.

Chapter 7: The Water Breaks

Back inside the Labor and Delivery room, Layla was just walking out of the bathroom, pushing the pole along laboriously. Her face was flushed, and she looked even more uncomfortable than earlier. Much as Marcus, she was having visions of holding her little girl. Looking down into her face and rocking her slowly, she spoke another prayer for her baby as she trudged along with the equipment, then suddenly paused. Her eyes opened up wide and she placed her hand to her stomach. She squinted and slightly cringed.

At this moment, Marcus was opening up the popcorn as he exited the snack room. Steam arose out of the torn bag, and the aroma of buttered popcorn tantalized his senses. He loved buttered

Popcorn. Any type of popcorn, for that matter. But the aroma was even more tantalizing considering he hadn't eaten since they'd left home, and he was starving. He tore open the bag, the scent of butter and salt wafting up to greet him. He blew on the top of the bag to cool it down, then proceeded to grab a handful of fluffy kernels as he walked up the hallway. He almost felt guilty about indulging in popcorn while his wife herself was undoubtedly hungry. But the feeling of guilt dissipated as he savored the warm, buttery goodness. He munched on the crunchy pieces, relishing in each bite. The reward of the perfectly popped kernels. The buttery goodness was worth it. At least he considered it to be. He took a sip of his drink to wash down the salty flavor as he now approached the door.

"Bae... I know you're gonna be mad at me but... this popcorn is deliciou..." His words broke off and abruptly ended as he beheld his wife standing motionless clutching the I.V. Her eyes were focusing down at the floor, prompting him to follow her gaze. There on the floor between her legs was fluids from her amniotic sac. As he stared at the puddle, she spoke out words that at this point were self-explanatory.

"My water broke," she stated matter-of-factly. Her voice was slightly above a whisper. Marcus was taken aback and frozen. His chest heaved and his facial expression evidenced the panic and anxiety he was experiencing. This was the moment that he and his wife had been anxiously awaiting for over 7 months. The baby that the two had mutually so desired was now, at this very moment, on the verge of entering into their lives. In a flash, he envisioned her little face looking up at him as the doctor delivered her. He thought about his drained wife's smile as she beholds her baby daughter. The time has come! "Ok. What should I do?" He pondered to himself. He glanced over at the monitor then reached for his wife's arm before realizing that going for the doctors or nurses would be the most feasible thing to do at this time. He didn't know whether he was coming or going.

"Ok. I'll uh... go get the nurse... the doctor. Not realizing that all he had to do was push the emergency call button. Ah... just... just wait right here babe... nurse!" He declared as he rushed out of the door. His words had been stammering as nervousness had completely enveloped him. His mind rushed as he jogged up the hallway towards the nurses' station. When he reached the front desk at the nurses' station, several of the nurses looked up from their work to behold him. Their expressions evidenced their curiosity at his abrupt approach, and no doubt noticed the look of anxiety that was evident on his face. One of the nurses - a middle-aged African American woman of voluptuous proportions - approached him with concern as he wiped his face.

"May I help you, sir?" She stated softly. The other nurses were still observing him. He wiped a nervous hand across his face and motioned down the hallway with his free hand.

"My wife's water just broke. She's in room 321." He explained. The nurse immediately went into motion and instructed one of the other nurses as she briskly came around the desk to follow him.

Nurses and their assistants scuttled back and forth through the foyer of the Labor and Delivery. A Caucasian doctor briefed a young male nurse as another female nurse squeaked away with a roll cart loaded down with equipment and other instruments necessary in the field of Phlebotomy. The doctor turned on his heels and placed his cell phone up to his ears as he disappeared into a room. Voices of nurses answering questions posed by patients seemed to mesh with the squeaking of nurses' Nike running shoes and the rustling of papers and monitor sounds.

Inside the delivery room, several doctors and nurses, along with their assistants, were fitting on their lime green scrubs. Layla's OB doctor finally arrived, placing gloves onto his hands as the nurse beside him opened up a cache of operating tools. Layla lay on the operating table, looking up into the overhead large bulb lamp. Her eyes seemed tired and worried. Marcus looked around the room at all of the doctors, nurses, and assistants before looking down into his wife's face. He knew she was worried. And he himself had never been so scared before. But he couldn't let her see the worry in his eyes. He squeezed her hand and kissed her on the hand, whispering that everything was going to be alright. But he actually had reserved feelings. These reserved feelings ranged from actually being concerned with his wife's physical and psychological well-being after delivery; to his concerns with the physical as well as mental health of their baby. Layla had had complications the entire pregnancy, and they both feared this having an effect on the unborn child. Both had done research into effects of premature births, and it had been unnerving to them both. These effects had ranged from the physical to psychological. The baby could be born with undeveloped lungs or other internal organs; or with psychosomatic syndromes that ranged from severe conditions such as Down Syndrome or Autism; to lesser but yet serious conditions like Muscular Dystrophy or other crippling and debilitating conditions. The thought of their little baby girl being diagnosed with either of these conditions had brought forth extensive anxiety to the couple. He tries to clear his mind from the possible reality and squeezes his wife's hand tighter.

Chapter 8: On the way

Layla's family and friends arrived at the hospital, praying alongside the hospital chaplin, Ms. Rose, and awaiting the baby's arrival. Dr. Glyn had come and told her that she would be prepped for her Cesarean. Layla was taken away and given an epidural. The assistants and nurses were now convening around the operating table. The doctor pulled up the protective mask over his face and motioned for the nurses' assistants. Marcus observed the doctor. He seemed to be highly experienced at delivering babies as was evidenced by the way she commandeered the delivery room. He gave instructions to the nurses and assistants, and Marcus watched as each complied, moving in unison, performing their own specified tasks. A hospital sheet was drawn up over Layla, and the nurses and assistants each tried to calm her. She was understandably nervous, and a nurse smiled at her as she ran a compassionate hand across her forehead and asked Layla, "had you guys picked out a name yet?" In a low tone, Layla replied, "Yes, we didn't know it was a girl until today, but we were prepared. It's a biblical name," but Layla tried to muster the baby's name from her lips, but before she could, a surge of pressure washed over her. "Aaaaaw!" She tensed slightly, feeling the sensation of intense pressure in her abdomen, though dulled by the effects of the epidural.

"You're gonna be ok, bae. OK?" The nurse assured. It was the nurse Marcus spoke with in the break room. Layla nodded her head and made an attempt at a smile that belied the worry in her eyes. She was anxious, and her chest heaved slightly. The doctor was at that moment whispering some more instructions to a nurse as another meticulously arranged the necessary utensils for the delivery. The doctor then made an announcement to ready the team of nurses and looked over at Marcus. Marcus himself was extremely nervous as the moment was now at hand. In moments the doctor would be holding his little baby girl. His angel. The anxiety grew with each second, and Layla was now squeezing his hand.

"Relax, bae," Marcus whispered. Layla's eyes were wide and darting. No doubt her mind was racing with apprehension or perhaps uncertainty of the degree of discomfort she was possibly facing. Or perhaps both. Marcus watched her lips tremble and recognized that she was saying something. It was unintelligible to him, but he surmised that she was saying a prayer. Marcus briefly closed his eyes and followed suit, sending up his own prayers for his wife's safety during the delivery, and for the safety of their little girl. When his eyes opened, Layla's eyes were squinted, and her face was a mask of worry. He then looked over to the doctor whose arms were beneath the teal blue hospital sheets. The nurses were all periodically and, in some instances, simultaneously coaching Layla through and offering their comforting words. Marcus examined the doctor's eyes through the glasses he wore, trying to discern any hint that the delivery was not somehow going well. But there were none.

"I have her head," he announced. Marcus looked to see and observed the little tiny reddened head emerging from under the sheet. Layla continued to grimace and moan in agony. Marcus' heart was now racing as he watched the doctor maneuver the baby from the birth canal. The entire body was now visible, and the first squeak of a cry sent sighs from the nurses around the delivery room.

Marcus' emotions were conflicting each other at this point, and his facial expressions were evidence of this fact. He was experiencing emotions of pride, relief, and joy as he took in the sight of his little baby girl being brought forth into this world; but at the same time overly concerned with the well-being of his wife. Though she cracked a relieved smile as she looked at the baby with loving eyes, Marcus knew that she was still anxious. He squeezed her hand tightly and once again kissed her on her head. She smiled at the quivering screaming newborn, and a tear rolled down her cheek. The couple continued to stare on lovingly as the doctor handed the baby over to the nurse assistants, who then expediently took the baby over to cut the umbilical cord and cleanse her of the afterbirth.

"She's here. Our baby girl is finally here," Marcus thought to himself as he watched the nurse assistants attending the baby. After a few moments, the baby was brought back over to the couple and placed into its mother's arms. There were signs and comments from the nurses and assistants who had now all removed their hospital masks. Marcus briefly stared around at all of them before beholding his wife in her moment of motherhood. She rocked her ever so gently, and Marcus studied her little face. She was now quiet and seemed to be comforted by her mother's gentle rocking and whispering. Marcus could not conceal his elation of the moment. He reached and touched the baby's hand giving her a gentle kiss on it. The baby's expression changed slightly, and her eyes moved beneath her eyelids, but she did not open them. He then kissed his wife and told her how much he loved her, all the while the backdrop of the hospital medical equipment overlapped the voices of nurses paging doctors, and the scampering squeaks of nurses' shoes and roll carts.

Shortly after taking their baby back for further observation, baby Hannah was taken to the Intensive Care Unit because of breathing difficulty. Layla and Marcus were given the bad news. The Hospital Chaplain, Mrs. Rose, came back into the room to pray with the new parents. After several hours passed, Layla called the NICU. With a trembling voice, she gave the nurse her passcode in order to get information on her newborn. The nurse told Layla that the baby was stable, and the Dr. would be in to speak with them shortly. The NICU doctor that was on call entered the room and spoke to Layla and Marcus. His name was Dr. Edwin. With a calm demeanor, the doctor gave an update on baby Hannah. "I just want the two of you to know that your little one is out of the woods. The NICU has excellent nurses and we will continue to monitor the baby closely and keep you updated throughout the day and night." There was a sigh of relief for the new parents. Tears flowed as they began to give thanks to God. After a week had passed, the baby was ready to be discharged from the hospital. Layla and Marcus had no problems with adjusting their home and lifestyle for their baby girl. Layla comes from a large family, and they were happy to assist the new parents.

8 months later

Chapter 9: Baby Blessings

The sound of the dryer could be heard thumping in the near distance as Layla, clad in a house robe and slippers, gathers more things from the laundry basket. It was 1:28 in the afternoon, and she was hurrying to load the last batch before her favorite soap opera began. She bundles up the clothes in her arm and walks briskly towards the washing machine. In another room, the baby was whining as if irritated. She turns her head towards the sound of the baby's voice emitting from the monitor on her kitchen counter. "Mommy's comin'. I got your bottle all ready, ok," Layla assures, though the baby couldn't understand her. She smiles as she opens up the top on the washing machine, then places the dirty clothes into the washer.

Meanwhile, Marcus holds a tape measure in his hand. His expression is one of determination as he examines the metal project before him. In the background, arcs of bright light emit, and the humming sounds of the metal fabricators overlap the sounds of electric grinders. Though his mind for the most part kept focused on the task at hand, ever so often his thoughts would drift to his wife and infant daughter. Images of her little face looking up at him as he held her in his arms would flash across the screen of his mind and cause a little twinge of a smile to emerge on his lips. He measures the metal plate, then marks off a line with chalk before reaching to grab his welding gun. Measuring the distance from plate to rod, he then flicks down the welding shield and begins to weld. The bright light was immense, and sparks spatter over the metal project. Then the sound of a whistle blows, signaling that it was time to punch the clock. It was quitting time.

Marcus raises up the shield onto the crown of his head and releases a sigh as he inspects his work. His face is covered in sweat, and he is perspiring profusely. He then begins to recoil his welding gun and replace all of his equipment as the other metal fabricators pass by him. Their faces, much like his, were masks of fatigue, covered in sweat, and the smell of musk and burnt metal wafts through the air. Marcus receives a pat on the shoulder from one of his co-workers and looks up into the smiling face of a middle-aged man. The man's warm smile was genuine, but his eyes belied the fatigue that was evident in him.

"You can go home and be with that little baby girl now," the co-worker says kindly. Marcus smiles and wipes sweat from his brow before responding. "Yes, sir, Mr. Charles. Been a long day, and I just want to get home, shower, and be with my little family." Mr. Charles smiles and pats him on the shoulder once again. "Yeah. It has been a rough one. Go home and be with your family. My children are grown. I just wanna get home to me a nice cold one and some leftover gumbo," Mr. Charles chuckles in his raspy gruff tone of voice. He had been working at the metal fabrication company longer than any of the other employees, with over forty years of experience, and had been welding since the 1960s. Originally from Texas, Mr. Charles had relocated to Louisiana as a rail yard engineer. Marcus had been working at the metal fab company with Mr. Charles for over three years, and the two had become very close. Marcus laughs at Mr. Charles's humor as the two walk out of the door amidst the clanging of equipment being put away and the chatter of workers eager to punch the clock and enjoy the freedom outside of the 100-degree-plus temperature of the tin building.

Chapter 10: Concerned Parents

Layla was now folding clothes and every so often glancing up at the television. The news was now airing, and she seemed to be interested in the broadcast. At the moment, a reporter was interviewing a middle-aged Caucasian lady who was giving in-depth information concerning prenatal care and birth defects. Layla listened intently as the woman went into detail about the various different kinds of defects that extended from the physical to the physiological and neural. As the interview continued, she would glance over into her little baby girl's face.

Layla's mind raced with apprehensive thoughts concerning the physical well-being of her baby girl, as well as the physiological defects that the doctor was informing of on the news broadcast. The baby seemed to be normal physically, but it was too early to determine whether or not she suffered from a debilitating psychological disorder. However, she had noticed that the baby didn't seem responsive to certain stimuli. This concerned her. She had mentioned this to her husband on a previous occasion, but the notion had been dismissed. After the news report on the healthcare of children in infancy switched to another topic, Layla clicked the button on the remote and surfed through the channels. Channels zoomed by as she stared almost blankly at the large screened TV. Her mind was no doubt still racing with those apprehensive thoughts concerning her baby girl. Frustrated, she shook her head and tossed down the remote onto the couch. She then cracked a smile and walked over towards the edge of the couch where the baby lay. She leaned over and picked her up into her arms and gently rocked her. She whispered something to her daughter then gave her a kiss. Moments later, her eyes averted from the non-cohesive stare of the baby to the gray sedan that was pulling into the driveway. Marcus was arriving back home from his long day at work.

Marcus closed the car door then took a quick inventory of the scenery surrounding his home. There were several children from different ethnic backgrounds either walking or riding their bicycles up and down the picturesque block as a light wind blew. He focused on one little girl in particular and smiled as he imagined his baby girl looking somewhat like the little girl at her age. His neighbors, a middle-aged african-american couple, waved and spoke to him as he walked towards the front door.

"Hi. How're you, Mr. and Mrs. Jackson?....that's good....oh, tired is all...ok." He returned the greeting, stifling a smile that belied the tiredness he felt. He released a sigh as he tried to locate the key for the front door. As he found the right key and was in the process of unlocking the door, to his surprise, it opened up and there in the doorway stood Layla. "Oh, hey babe." He greeted. The two kissed briefly then he entered through the front door as Layla closed it behind them.

As he took off his light jacket, he took a deep whiff at the aroma that was tantalizing his senses. In between the house chores, Layla had prepared a meal of okra and white rice. "Smells good. What did you cook, babe?" He inquired. Layla was in the process of removing the apron as the question was posed.

"Your favorite. Sausage, shrimp, okra, white rice and cornbread. Do you want your plate now, or after you bathe?" She inquired.

"Oh. Not now, babe. I gotta go wash this soot off me. How's our beautiful baby girl?" He asked as his attention focused on the baby lying in her crib. Layla looked over toward the baby as Marcus walked over to touch her hand. Layla rushed over to the crib to reach Marcus the hand sanitizer before he touched the baby. "Already washed 'em!" Marcus began to gently take his daughter from her crib. The baby's little mouth pursed, but her expression never changed. Thoughts of concern briefly ran across Marcus' mind, but instead of alarming Layla, he smiled at little 'Hannah Grace' and began to 'baby talk' to her..."hey, my little angel, how's daddy's favorite little girl doing?" Layla looked over at her husband and smiled. "She has you wrapped around those little fingers already." Marcus nodded in agreement. He carefully placed Hannah down on her back. "There's nothing I wouldn't do for you and my baby girl," Marcus stated. "I want the best for her, the best for us." "Whatever God has for us, is for us. So don't get yourself in a bind trying to give us the world; life is more than material possessions. All I want is for Hannah to be healthy, healthy!" Layla said, with a quivering voice.

Layla stopped what she was doing and ran into her bedroom. She then fell onto the bed and began to cry. Marcus ran after her."Babe," he said in a calm voice, "what's all this about, what's wrong?""Nothing," she stated, with tears rolling down her face. "Maybe I'm just having some postpartum depression." "I know that I'm not your doctor, but isn't it a little too late to be experiencing that?" He asked with concern. "I, I don't know. I'll just call my doctor's office in the morning and ask." But Layla's concern was not for herself. Her concerns were for her daughter. However, she did not share concerns with her husband because she thought she may have been overreacting.

Chapter 11: Doctor's Appointment

The next morning, Layla called the doctor's office, but it wasn't her doctor that she called; it was Hannah's pediatrician's office. The nurse informed Layla that it was time for Hannah Grace's checkup. "Be there in the morning," Layla told Dr. Duke, who has specialized in Pediatrics for over 30 years. Dr. Duke had also been Layla's pediatrician when she was a child, so she trusted him, but most importantly to her, she trusted God!

The morning had come, and an anxious Layla was preparing her husband's breakfast before he left for work. "Mmmm Mmm, smells good bae," Marcus said as he was walking down the staircase toward the kitchen. "All for you hun, I'm eating light this morning, gotta get rid of some of this baby fat," Layla replied. He looked at Layla and smiled, "More of you to love." "Yeah right!" Layla said, with a smirk. "I wasn't too drugged to see how you were watching those petite young RN's while I was giving birth, I saw ya." "Bae, I must admit, there is another female that I have eyes for," Layla looked at Marcus with a puzzling expression... "And she's right here!" he said as he was holding Hannah Grace, his beautiful little brown-skinned girl in the air. When she was thrown in the air, the scent from her diaper blew across her dad's nose... "Eeew, and she smells like poo! She's all yours now," he said jokingly. "That's about right, sure, give her to me when she's full of it," Layla said with a smile, "but I'll take her, I'll take my baby girl any time." Marcus finished his breakfast and then kissed his wife and daughter before hurrying out of the door to work. Layla let out a sigh of relief as she watched Marcus walk out of the door and start his car because she was doing her best to combat her true emotions. "Almost that time baby girl, we got to get to Dr. Duke's office and get you checked out," Layla said, talking to Hannah in a soft, concerned voice. Hannah looked up at her mother and smiled, as though she actually knew what she was saying. Layla placed Hannah in her carrier, safely buckled her in, and walked slowly to the SUV. Several scenarios played in her mind about how the doctor's appointment would go. As Layla got into the driver's seat of her vehicle, she paused for a moment with a blank stare. "Time to ride baby girl." Layla buckled her seatbelt as she searched for track five on her CD player. Her favorite gospel song started to play. After about two minutes into the song, the words seemed to overtake her, and cold tears ran down her face. "Let me pull myself together. I don't want to walk into the doctor's office with swollen eyes and smeared makeup," Layla said to herself.

Layla and Hannah had made it to the pediatrician's office. Before getting out of the car, Layla made a phone call to her mother. Layla was an only child with very few friends, so she relied on her mother's advice often. "Ma," she said, as she could hear her mother's voice on the other end with her Southern accent. "What's wrong na?" her mother inquired. "Nothing, nothing much. I'm just sitting here in the parking lot at the doctor's office with Hannah, and I'm dreading going in." "Where is your Faith?" her mother asked with a strong voice. "I have faith, but this is my baby girl, my only child. "Could you just pray with me before I go in?" "I was praying for you before you called me, so get off this phone and get your tail in the office before you miss my grandbaby's appointment!" "Ok, ok, ma," Layla stated as she wiped her face! Layla entered the building. The office was packed with screaming infants and toddlers. While signing in, she looked around and saw one of her old high school friends. "Erika! Haven't seen you in years!" "Hey Layla," Erika replied as she was cradling her daughter and waiting to be called to the back. "Good to see ya! Beautiful girl you have there. And you have a beautiful girl as well." The two ladies didn't have time to catch up; they only got the chance to exchange numbers before Erika and her baby were called to the back. Layla impatiently took a seat. She placed Hannah Grace on the floor in front of her while reaching into the diaper bag and searching for Hannah's favorite stuffed animal and rattle. Layla placed the white stuffed lamb in Hannah's hand. She then shook the pink rattle up and down to try and entertain her baby until they were called to the back. After about 20 minutes of waiting in the crowded noisy office, there was a voice over the intercom, "Hannah Evans!" called the voice over the intercom. Layla jumped up from her seat, grabbing the diaper bag and carrier. A stumbling Layla was greeted at the door by a smiling nurse. "Hey mom, go three doors down and take a right." Layla walked toward the exam room with the assistant behind her. After getting settled in the room, the nurse's assistant began asking questions about Hannah's physical health and development. "Are there any other concerns that you may have for your little one that the doctor needs to address when he comes in, Mrs. Evans?" "Ah, Yes...yes there is," Layla explained her concerns to the young nurse as she awaited Dr. Duke's arrival. "I understand your concerns for your daughter, but try not to worry so much. She's still very young right now." The nurse then pricked Hannah's finger for blood work. Hannah only primps her mouth, not making much of a sound. The nurse looked at Hannah with a perplexed look, but to keep from alarming Layla, she quickly changed her expression. "Na, that's a big girl! Didn't cry a bit. Ok mom, I'll get this sample to the lab so the doctor can have it before he comes in. It won't be long." The nurse left the room. Layla began to cradle Hannah, singing the baby's favorite tune. "Yes Jesus loves me, yes Jesus loves me, Yes Jesus loves me, for the bible tells me so." Hannah didn't respond too much, but she would often seem to respond to the song with 'cooing' as though she was trying to sing along with her mother. "I hear you trying to sing along with me," Layla stated with laughter. "But you're not quite ready just yet." The slight communication between Layla and Hannah was interrupted when a medium-built, elderly African American doctor walked into the room. It was Dr. Duke. "Good morning, Mrs. Evans." "Good morning, Doctor Duke," replied Layla as she sat Hannah up onto the table to be examined. "Well, looka here, 8 months already," Dr. Duke said, smiling. "That's right, my baby girl is 8 months old now." "What seems to be the problem today, is she just here for her 8-month check-up?" The doctor inquires. "She's here because it's time for her check-up, and I also have concerns about her growth and development." "Very well then, let me take a look at her, and after I examine her, then you can tell me about your concerns." Dr. Duke took the stethoscope and began listening to the baby's heart and lungs. "She has a strong heart, and her lungs are clear." The doctor then took the otoscope and looked into the ears and throat of baby Hannah. "No signs of infection, and her blood work was also negative. Your baby seems healthy, just like you were when you came into my office around this age." "Now what are the concerns that you have about her growth and development?" With a raspy voice, Layla replied, "Umm, I've just noticed a few things, a few things that concern me!" "Well, Hannah is eight months now, and I just kinda figured that she should be a little bit more aware and verbal by now. My cousin's twins are the same age as Hannah, and… Let me stop you right here, Mrs. Evans, ah, Layla. You can't compare your daughter to your cousin's children; even if you had an older child, you wouldn't be able to compare the two siblings, simply because babies learn and grow at different paces." "But I talk and sing to her all the time," Layla stated, still feeling concerned. "Ok, Layla, her next appointment is scheduled for 4 months, so try not to worry. But if she is having any problems prior to her appointment, feel free to bring her in." "Ok, doc," Layla expressed in a relieved tone. Layla placed baby Hannah into her carrier and headed to her vehicle. As she buckled Hannah into the carseat, she kissed her on her hand, got into her SUV and drove off.

Chapter 12: New Career

After leaving the doctor's office Layla turned her radio to the Gospel station that she always listens to. "Oh, I love this song," Layla began to sing and hum along with the music on the radio. "Hmm hmm... steps, dear Lord, lead me... every day, send your... I pray…" As Layla was singing, and had come to a red light, she looked back at Hannah only to see a big smile on her face, as though she was trying to sing along with her. "You singing gospel with mommy?" Layla asked with a smile. Tears fell down Layla's face as she briefly gazed at her daughter seemingly trying to sing along with her. Just then, Layla heard a loud honk! The person driving behind flipped her off and blew their horn because the light had turned green. "Uuuh, that bas… Sorry, Lord. Bridle my tongue," she said, speaking to God with laughter. "You know, Lord, that I'm not quite there yet." Layla took the scenic route and drove slowly because driving seemed to help ease her mind. After driving for an extra 30 minutes, Layla and Hannah had finally made it home. "We're here, sweetie." Hannah had done like most babies do when they are riding comfortably in the back seat. She had fallen asleep. Layla took her sleeping baby into the house and placed her in the crib. As she turned on the lullaby music, she heard Marcus coming through the front door. "Hey, bae," Marcus spoke as though he hadn't seen his wife and daughter in months. "Why are you so excited?" Layla asked. "Just happy to see my beautiful girls," Marcus exclaimed. "And... And what?" she asked curiously. "I have another job offer." "Another Job?" "I guess that's great, bae! We could sure use the money because Hannah eats like a piglet! But why were you so hesitant to tell me, what's the catch?" Layla asked with a concerned expression. Marcus looked into his wife's eyes, hesitant to tell her all the details of the offer. "Well, bae?" "It would require me to go out of town to train for about three months." "Three Months!" Layla asked in an elevated tone. "How am I supposed to care for Hannah by myself?" "Well, you could ask your mother to stay with you until I come back from training. You know she would love to stay here with you and spoil Hannah while I'm away." Layla sat down in her recliner with a blank stare. She looked up at Marcus, and asked, "What about me? You know I don't like being away from you for long periods of time." "Baaae," Marcus responded. "You know I don't like being away from you either." Marcus then sat in the recliner with his wife to comfort her by putting his arms around her and sharing a passionate kiss. The two of them discussed the details of the job offer and decided it would be financially beneficial. As they fell into each other's arms and began to give in to their sexual desires, there was a noise in the background. Waaa! The two of them then turned towards Hannah, and then looked back at each other saying simultaneously, "Not so perfect timing." "Oh well, maybe later," Layla stated. "It's bath time!" Layla gave Hannah an early bath in hopes that she and Marcus could sit down and talk more about his new job offer and maybe spend a little quality time together. Hannah loved to take warm baths. They seemed to soothe her, and afterwards, Hannah fell right to sleep. All sorts of scenarios were going through Layla's mind about not having Marcus around and basically raising Hannah Grace on her own. After taking a relaxing bath herself, Layla seemed to be a little bit more relaxed. She knew that she would eventually be okay with Marcus leaving and that her mom and family would be there to assist her. Marcus was already in the bedroom watching television, so she went in to lay beside him. "Marcus," she said. "What, bae?" Layla went on to say that she knows that she and the baby will be fine and that she has the support she needs while he is away. Marcus put his arms around his wife and began to comfort her as he usually does. The two of them begin to passionately kiss, but before things get heated, Marcus falls asleep. Layla looks at Marcus, rolling her eyes at him in disappointment. "Guess I have to get used to not getting any," she stated.

Chapter 13: Birthday Blues

"Four months later, Marcus had just returned home from offshore training in time for Hannah's first birthday party. Layla greeted her husband with a warm embrace. "Oh my God, I've missed you so much! I didn't think that you were going to make it in time for the party! Too bad you weren't here to help with the preparations," Layla stated jokingly.

"Well, I sent the money for it all, didn't I?" Marcus replied.

"Yes, you did, baby, and I hope that there is plenty more where that came from, because I could use some retail therapy."

"So where is daddy's big girl? I can't wait to hold her!" Marcus said anxiously.

"Come on, I can't wait for her to see that handsome face of yours!" The couple hurried to the family room where Hannah was sitting on the floor, staring at the big pink balloons that Layla purchased for the party.

"Haaaana," Marcus started with a calm voice, to keep from startling her. Hannah kept playing with the balloon as though her dad wasn't squatting down beside her. "You're not happy to see daddy?" Marcus looked away and then looked into his wife's face. "Bae? Shouldn't she be more receptive to me by now? Shouldn't she be smiling and responding to her name by now?"

"I was going to discuss all of this with you, but it will have to wait until after the party."

"I'm not in the mood for a party," Marcus stated. "I'm just not in the mood now!" Marcus went into the bedroom and softly closed the door behind him.

The guests and their children started to arrive. "Happy Birthday!" The children screamed upon arrival, causing Hannah to briefly grab her ears but Hannah was still fascinated with the balloon she had been playing with earlier. "Honey, can you come out of the room please, the guests have arrived." Layla states. Marcus hesitantly came out of the room to congregate with the birthday guests.

"It's great to have you safely back home, just in time for your daughter's first birthday," remarked one of the parents. Marcus smiled and replied, "Thank God, I'm grateful too."

While Layla busily hosted the party, Hannah appeared unenthusiastic about the birthday crowd. The constant noise around her made her constantly cover her ears, raising concern among the guests. "Does she have an ear infection?" inquired one guest. "No," Layla reassured, "I think she's just sleepy; she didn't rest well last night."

As the party concluded after a few hours, an overwhelmed Hannah and her parents were relieved. Layla's mom offered to stay behind and help clean up, saying, "I'll stay in the guest room and attend to Hannah tonight while you two get some rest."

Layla, with a tired tone, expressed, "Rest? What is that?"

"Come on, honey, listen to your mother," Marcus replied.

After cleaning, Layla and Marcus headed into their bedroom, where they collapsed on the couch. "Put 'em up here," Marcus suggested, proceeding to massage Layla's feet. "That feels wonderful," she sighed.

As they tried to relax, their minds dwelled on the day's events and concerns for their baby girl. "What if Hannah..." Marcus began a question, but Layla swiftly cut him off, saying, "Don't even think it, don't even speak it."

Their hearts heavy with worry, they found solace in each other's company, hoping for better days ahead for their beloved Hannah.

Chapter 14: A Mother's Concern

The next chapter opens with Layla and Marcus preparing for Hannah's 1-year-old check-up. The atmosphere in the house is tense, and a lingering worry hangs in the air. Layla carefully dresses Hannah in a cute little Saints outfit, adorned with a pink ribbon in her hair. Marcus looks on, concern etched on his face.

As they head to the doctor's office, the autumn wind outside whispers through the car windows, adding an eerie calmness to the atmosphere. The leaves dance on the ground, mirroring the turmoil in Layla's heart.

The waiting room at the pediatrician's office is adorned with colorful posters and toys. However, Hannah seems disinterested, fixating on a spinning mobile hanging above her. Layla exchanges a glance with Marcus, both silently acknowledging the growing signs that something might be wrong.

When the nurse calls Hannah's name, they enter the examination room. The nurse, a warm and empathetic asian woman, greets the family. She begins the routine check-up, measuring Hannah's height, weight, and examining her overall health.

As the examination progresses, the nurse starts asking about Hannah's developmental milestones. Layla hesitates before admitting, "She's not talking yet. We were hoping she would start saying a few words by now."

The nurse maintains a comforting demeanor, understanding the delicate nature of the situation. She engages with Hannah, attempting to elicit responses, but Hannah remains non-responsive. The nurse informs them that Dr. Duke will be in shortly and she swiftly exits the room. Dr. Duke enters the room and begins to examine Hannah. After the examination he turns and look at Layla and Marcus.

"Layla and Marcus, I want to discuss some observations I've made during the examination," the doctor begins, choosing his words carefully. "Hannah is displaying certain signs that are indicative of autism spectrum disorder. She's only one but it's crucial for us to explore this further and consider early intervention."

Layla's eyes well up with tears, and Marcus tightens his grip on her hand. The doctor goes on to explain the signs they've observed, such as limited eye contact, lack of response to her name, and the absence of spoken words. She reassures them that early intervention can make a significant difference in helping Hannah reach her full potential.

After the doctor's appointment, Layla and Marcus sit in the car, grappling with a mix of emotions. Layla sits in the back seat with Hannah clutching Hannah's tiny hand. Marcus starts the engine, but neither speaks for a while.

"We'll get through this together," Marcus finally breaks the silence, his voice unwavering. Layla nods, a determined look in her eyes. They drive home with a newfound commitment to support their daughter in every way possible.

The chapter concludes with Layla, in the dim light of the evening, kneeling beside Hannah's crib during naptime, whispering a heartfelt prayer for strength, guidance, and unwavering love as they navigate this new and challenging journey with their precious daughter

Chapter 15: Faith and Employment

The chapter opens with a somber Sunday morning. Layla and Marcus arrive at church, carrying the weight of Hannah's recent diagnosis with them. They approach pastor Joseph, their faces reflective of their struggle, and request his and the congregation's prayers for Hannah's improvement. The pastor, sensing their distress, assures them of the church's support and invites everyone to join in prayer after the sermon.

As pastor Joseph and the congregation pray for Hannah's well-being, the atmosphere is charged with a mix of empathy and hope. Layla, with tears streaming down her face, finds solace in the collective prayers of her church family. Marcus and her mom stands by her side, a pillar of strength.

After the service concluded, Layla and Marcus meet again with their pastor for words of guidance and comfort. The pastor encourages them to continue relying on their faith and emphasizes the importance of seeking support from their church community during difficult times.

Feeling the need to contribute more to the family, Layla decides to take on employment at a fashion clothing store. The job offers a flexible schedule, allowing her to balance work and caring for Hannah. Marcus, too, decides to return to work, understanding the financial strain the family is under.

With Layla working part-time, the family faces the challenge of finding suitable care for Hannah. Layla's mom, Mary, who is disabled and unable to provide full-time care, suggests a nearby childcare facility she heard about. Layla, hesitant but with limited options, decides to give it a try, hoping that the caregivers at the center will be able to support Hannah's needs.

The first day at the childcare center is emotionally taxing for Layla. As she hesitantly leaves Hannah in the care of strangers, uncertainty and worry cloud her thoughts. Her mom tries to reassure her, emphasizing the importance of maintaining faith that things will work out.

However, as weeks pass, signs emerge that all is not well at the childcare center. Layla notices subtle changes in Hannah's behavior—she becomes more withdrawn, avoids eye contact, and exhibits signs of fear. Concerned, Layla begins to investigate and discovers alarming evidence of possible physical and verbal abuse inflicted upon her vulnerable daughter at the childcare.

Fueled by a mother's instinct to protect, Layla confronts the childcare center staff, demanding answers and accountability. Unknowing to Layala, one of the other workers who happen to be passing by the classroom door during nap time witnessed Hannah being taunted and physically abused for not going to sleep during nap time by a new employee. The employee seemed to have bruises on herself as well. Bruises that may have been caused by her boyfriend who has been seen causing minor disturbances in the childcare parking lot. The new employee was referred by a friend of the owner, so the background check that is required before hire was never done.

Chapter 16: Unveiling the Truth

With Marcus still out of town for work, Layla faces the challenge of addressing the concerns about Hannah's well-being at the childcare center on her own. She knows she needs answers and reassurance about her child's safety. Layla's mother, Mary, is determined to accompany her daughter to the childcare center, ready to assertively voice her concerns.

As they walk into the facility, the air is tense with anticipation. The childcare workers, sensing the gravity of the situation, exchange uneasy glances. Layla, though not naturally confrontational, tightens her grip on Mary's arm, drawing strength from her mother's supportive presence.

Approaching the center's supervisor, Layla takes a deep breath, trying to find the right words. Mary, however, wastes no time in expressing her concerns with a straightforward approach.

"Miss, we've been hearing some troubling things about what's happening here. Our little Hannah seems different since she started coming here. We need answers, and we need them now," Mary asserts, her tone unwavering.

Layla, grateful for her mother's assertiveness, nods in agreement, reinforcing the urgency of their concerns. The supervisor, taken aback but recognizing the seriousness of the situation, invites them into a private meeting room.

In the meeting, Layla delicately describes the changes she has noticed in Hannah's behavior. She emphasizes the need for transparency and open communication about her daughter's experiences while in their care. Mary, less patient and more direct, demands immediate action and accountability.

As the supervisor, Ms Tiffany, responds, offering explanations and assurances, Layla carefully gauges the sincerity in her words. Mary, however, cuts through the what she considers bullshit, demanding concrete steps to address the issues at hand.

"Enough talking. We need to see where my grandbaby spends her day and who's taking care of her," Mary insists, her determination evident in her eyes.

Ms. Tiffany reluctantly agrees to a tour of the facility. Layla and Mary observe the childcare workers interacting with the children, paying close attention to Hannah's demeanor and any signs of mistreatment.

As the tour progresses, Layla's concerns are partially alleviated, but Mary remains vigilant. After the tour, they reconvene with the supervisor to discuss their findings.

Layla, now more assertive, requests a detailed plan for addressing the issues raised and insists on increased transparency between the center and parents. Mary, satisfied with the course of action outlined, makes it clear that she will be monitoring the situation closely.

The chapter concludes with Layla and Mary leaving the childcare center with Hannah, the weight of the situation still heavy on their hearts. Layla, now more determined than ever to protect her daughter, reflects on the strength she found within herself and the unwavering support of her mother during this challenging time.

Chapter 17: Healing and Decisions

Layla, burdened by the possibility of Hannah's mistreatment at the daycare center, musters the courage to share the troubling news with Marcus during a phone call. As the words spill out, Marcus feels a mix of anger, worry, and helplessness on the other end of the line. He decides to cut his offshore job short, realizing that his place is beside his family during this challenging time.

When Marcus arrives home, the atmosphere is heavy with tension. Layla is visibly distraught, her eyes swollen from tears shed in solitude. The couple shares a long, silent embrace, finding solace in the familiarity of each other's presence.

"Layla," Marcus begins gently, breaking the silence. "We'll get through this together. I promise."

In the days that follow, Layla takes a brave step toward healing and contacts a mental health counselor. The decision to seek counseling is a joint one with Marcus, recognizing the toll the recent events have taken on Layla's mental well-being. The counselor provides a safe space for Layla to express her fears, frustrations, and anxieties, offering guidance and coping mechanisms.

As Layla begins her counseling sessions, Marcus takes on a more active role in managing the situation with Hannah. He spends quality time with their daughter, fostering a sense of security and trust. Marcus also starts researching in-home sitters, recognizing the need for a more controlled and nurturing environment for Hannah.

During one of Layla's counseling sessions, Marcus joins her to discuss their options. The counselor facilitates a conversation about the impact of recent events on the family and explores potential solutions. Layla expresses her reluctance to continue with traditional childcare and shares her desire for a more personalized and secure setting for Hannah.

"After everything that's happened, I just can't bear the thought of leaving Hannah in someone else's care," Layla admits, her voice trembling with emotion.

Marcus nods in understanding, his hand finding hers for support. "We'll find a solution, Layla. Together."

After much deliberation, Layla and Marcus make the decision to opt for an in-home sitter who can provide dedicated care and a familiar environment for their daughter. The couple interview potential sitters, seeking someone experienced and compassionate, who can understand and accommodate Hannah's unique needs.

As the new routine takes shape, Layla continues her counseling sessions to navigate the emotional aftermath of the daycare incident. The couple finds solace in each other, realizing the strength of their bond and their shared commitment to Hannah's well-being.

The chapter concludes with a sense of renewal as the in-home sitter becomes an integral part of their daily life. Layla, supported by counseling, begins to rebuild her confidence, and Marcus is determined to create a safe haven for their family. Together, they embark on a journey of healing, determined to provide the best possible future for their beloved Hannah.

Chapter 18: Navigating Kindergarten

As years passed, Hannah embarked on her journey into kindergarten, and Layla and Marcus found themselves facing new challenges. The school had a special program for children with autism, providing a supportive environment for Hannah's unique needs. However, as they soon discovered, the transition to kindergarten brought about a set of unforeseen struggles.

Hannah, now a petite five-year-old, her slender frame adorned with long, ebony locks cascading over her shoulders, accentuated by tiny brown freckles dotting her delicate features. She stood at the threshold of the kindergarten classroom, her attire adorned in a charming uniform, her small fingers tightly clutching the straps of her backpack, a manifestation of her apprehension and excitement.

Layla and Marcus, her devoted parents, shared a glance filled with a potent blend of pride and nervous anticipation. Their intertwined hands served as a tangible display of solidarity as they accompanied their daughter into the bustling room, where she was greeted warmly by her new teachers. The air was charged with a mixture of emotions as they watched Hannah take her first steps into the world of formal education, a poignant milestone in her journey of growth and discovery.

"Are you ready, sweetheart?" Layla whispered, brushing a stray hair from Hannah's forehead. Hannah nodded, her expression a blend of excitement and nervousness.

Before the challenges arose, Hannah's days at school were characterized by the gentle rhythm of routine and the comfort of familiar faces. As a nonverbal child on the autism spectrum, she navigated the bustling halls with a quiet determination, her shy demeanor a shield against the overwhelming stimuli of the world around her.

In her kindergarten classroom, Hannah found solace in the structured environment crafted by her dedicated teachers, Shelly and Naome. With their patient guidance and understanding, they created a safe space where Hannah could retreat into her own world, free from the pressures of communication and social interaction.

Despite her hesitance to engage with others, Hannah's presence brought a sense of calm to the classroom. With her soft-spoken nature and gentle demeanor, she moved through the day with a quiet grace, her eyes alight with curiosity as she observed her surroundings with keen interest.

Shelly and Naome, experienced educators well-versed in supporting children on the autism spectrum, tailored their approach to meet Hannah's unique needs. With patience and empathy, they provided the scaffolding necessary for Hannah to navigate the complexities of the classroom environment, offering gentle encouragement and support every step of the way.

In this nurturing environment, Hannah found moments of peace and tranquility amidst the chaos of the school day. Whether it was tracing shapes in the sand table or listening to the soothing melodies of a quiet corner, she discovered pockets of joy in the simple pleasures of everyday life.

As the days unfolded, Hannah's quiet presence became a source of inspiration to her teachers and classmates alike. Though she may not have spoken a word, her silent strength and unwavering determination spoke volumes, a testament to the resilience and beauty of the human spirit.

"After weeks had passed, Shelly and Naome, convened a meeting with Marcus and Layla to address Hannah's recent behavioral challenges. Despite their nurturing and structured approach, Hannah's behavior had become increasingly aggressive towards both her teachers and classmates, prompting concern from her parents.

"I appreciate you both taking the time to meet with us," Layla said, her voice tinged with worry as she glanced at Marcus. "We're eager to understand how we can best support Hannah at home and at school."

Marcus nodded in agreement, his expression mirroring Layla's concern. "Yes, we want to make sure we're doing everything we can to help Hannah thrive in both environments."

Shelly nodded empathetically, her warm gaze fixed on the couple. "We understand your concerns, and we're here to work together in finding solutions," she said reassuringly. "We've been closely monitoring Hannah's behavior at school, and we have some observations to share."

Naome chimed in, her voice gentle yet firm. "Despite our best efforts, Hannah's aggression seems to be escalating in the classroom. We believe it's crucial for us to collaborate on strategies to address this behavior effectively."

This adjustment ensures that both home and school environments are considered in supporting Hannah's well-being and addressing her behavioral challenges.

Layla and Marcus listened intently as the teachers outlined their observations and proposed strategies for managing Hannah's aggression. As the discussion unfolded, a sense of relief washed over them, knowing they had a dedicated team of educators supporting their daughter's journey. Together, they delved into the complexities of Hannah's needs, united in their commitment to helping her navigate the challenges ahead.

"We're in this together," one of the teachers said reassuringly. "We'll do whatever it takes to help Hannah succeed."

In addition to the teachers, the school brought in a behavioral specialist to assess Hannah's behaviors more comprehensively. The specialist observed her interactions, analyzed triggers, and developed an individualized plan to support her emotional and behavioral development.

Layla and Marcus, though reassured by the school's commitment, were faced with the emotional toll of witnessing their daughter struggle. They attended workshops and support groups offered by the school to gain insights into managing aggressive behaviors associated with autism. The parents found solace in connecting with other families facing similar challenges, sharing experiences, and learning from one another.

The narrative explored the complexities of balancing expectations for socialization and academic progress with the need to provide tailored support for Hannah. Layla and Marcus grappled with a range of emotions, from frustration to determination, as they navigated this new chapter in their daughter's life.

As the chapter unfolded, the focus shifted towards implementing the strategies recommended by the behavioral specialist and teachers. Layla and Marcus worked closely with the school to reinforce consistency between home and classroom environments, providing a united front of support for Hannah.

The chapter concluded with a sense of hope as Layla, Marcus, and the school collaborated to create a customized plan that accommodated Hannah's unique needs. The journey through kindergarten became an opportunity for growth, understanding, and resilience for the Evans family.

Chapter 19: Supermarket Struggles

The chapter begins with the Evans family—Marcus, Layla, and Hannah—venturing into a bustling grocery store. The fluorescent lights flicker overhead, and the chatter of shoppers echoes through the aisles. Hannah, holding onto the cart, appears overwhelmed by the sensory overload. Her eyes dart around, and she clutches the sides of her head.

As they navigate through the store, Hannah's anxiety intensifies. The hum of the refrigerators, the chatter of other shoppers, and the colorful displays all become too much for her to process. In her frustration, Hannah starts to act out, kicking her legs and letting out high-pitched cries.

Layla, ever the patient mother, attempts to soothe Hannah, gently whispering comforting words and stroking her hair. Marcus, however, grows visibly frustrated, the strain of dealing with Hannah's outbursts apparent on his face.

"Come on, Hannah, you need to calm down," Marcus exhorts, his tone edging towards impatience. Layla shoots him a pleading glance, silently asking for understanding.

As they continue down the aisles, Hannah's agitation escalates further. In a sudden burst of frustration, she lashes out, attacking her parents. Marcus, struggling to maintain composure, sternly tells Hannah to stop. Layla intervenes, trying to shield both Marcus and Hannah from each other's reactions.

The situation becomes a crucible of emotions. Layla, torn between the challenging reality of Hannah's condition and her unwavering faith, silently prays for strength. Marcus, feeling the weight of the public scene and the difficulties of raising a child with autism, begins to lose his patience.

The episode prompts a crucial conversation between Marcus and Layla in a quieter section of the store. They grapple with their differing coping mechanisms and the strain on their relationship. Marcus expresses his frustration, admitting that he's finding it increasingly difficult to handle Hannah's unpredictable behavior.

Layla, still grounded in her faith, encourages Marcus to seek support and understanding. "We need to be a united front for Hannah," she says, gently reminding him of the importance of patience and empathy.

In the checkout line, Layla, Marcus, and Hannah find themselves surrounded by curious stares. Layla, unfazed by the judgmental glances, continues to comfort Hannah, whispering words of reassurance. Marcus, though visibly stressed, takes a deep breath, realizing the need for better strategies in handling such situations.

The chapter concludes with the family leaving the store, the echoes of Hannah's outburst lingering in the air. As they load the groceries into the car, Marcus and Layla exchange a silent acknowledgment of the challenges they face. The narrative sets the stage for the family to explore new ways of supporting Hannah and strengthening their resilience as they navigate the complexities of raising a child with autism.

Chapter 20: Seeking Support

As the demands of caring for Hannah intensify, Layla observes a visible change in Marcus. His exhaustion is etched on his face, and he's become increasingly distant. Layla recognizes the strain he's under, both at work and at home, and decides it's time to seek help.

One Sunday after church, Layla approaches their pastor, a trusted confidant who has been a pillar of support for the Evans family for over thirty years. She shares her concerns about Marcus, his growing distance, and the challenges they face with Hannah's care. The pastor and his wife listens attentively, his compassionate gaze reflecting understanding.

"Layla, we're here for you both. It's important to address these challenges together," the pastor reassures her. Recognizing the need for spiritual guidance, Layla gathers the courage to ask for counseling.

The pastor, acknowledging the strain Marcus is facing, suggests seeking spiritual counseling as a way to navigate through these challenges. "Counseling can be a powerful tool to help both of you cope with the complexities of raising a child with special needs," he advises.

With the pastor Franklin's encouragement, Layla approaches Marcus about the idea of counseling. Marcus, initially resistant, eventually agrees, realizing the toll that the responsibilities of work and caring for Hannah have taken on him.

Layla also turns to her supportive network of friends and family. Recognizing that the journey of caring for a disabled child can be physically and emotionally draining, they step forward to offer assistance. Jane and Melissa offer to spend time with Hannah, and family members volunteer to help with household tasks. This network of support becomes a crucial lifeline for Layla and Marcus.

Spiritual counseling sessions the pastor and his wife provide Layla and Marcus with a safe space to express their individual challenges and concerns. A professional counselor, Mrs. King, offers guidance on effective communication, coping mechanisms, and strategies for managing stress.

As Layla navigates the complexities of being a caregiver and a supportive partner, she finds strength in the unity of her network. Friends take Hannah for outings, providing Layla with moments of respite. Family members assist with daily tasks, creating a more manageable routine.

Layla reflects on the power of community and the importance of seeking help when needed. She learns to balance the roles of caregiver, wife, and mother, realizing that her own well-being is vital for the well-being of her family.

The chapter concludes with Layla and Marcus attending counseling together, a step towards healing and strengthening their bond. The supportive network around them continues to play a crucial role in lightening the load, fostering resilience, and reaffirming the value of community in the face of life's challenges.

Chapter 21: A Picnic with Destin

Hannah's heart danced with anticipation as she followed her parents towards the park. The sun was shining brightly, casting a warm glow over the lush greenery. The gentle breeze carried the sweet scent of flowers, promising a delightful day ahead.

As they found a serene spot beneath a sprawling oak tree, Hannah's parents laid out a colorful picnic blanket. Hannah watched eagerly as her mother unpacked sandwiches, fruit, and her favorite chocolate chip cookies from the picnic basket. The vibrant array of food made her mouth water with excitement.

Beside her, Hannah's friend Destin and his little sister's Treasure and Kira appeared, their faces lighting up with a bright smile. Destin was a bundle of energy, always eager to play and explore. He didn't care that Hannah seemed different—he loved her just the same.

With a gleeful shout, Destin bounded towards Hannah, his laughter echoing through the park. He reached out a hand, inviting her to join him in a game of tag. Despite her initial hesitation, Hannah couldn't resist the infectious joy sparkling in Destin's eyes.

"It's ok Hannah, you can go." Marcus stated, looking up at Destin with a smile. With a grin, Hannah nodded, her heart racing with excitement. Together, they darted through the park, their laughter blending with the rustle of leaves and the chirping of birds. In that moment, Hannah felt a sense of freedom she rarely experienced—the freedom to be herself, without fear or judgment.

After their game of tag, Destin eagerly led Hannah to the swings, pushing her higher and higher with each joyful push. Hannah's laughter filled the air as she soared through the sky, the wind whipping through her hair. Beside her, Destin cheered her on, his encouragement a constant source of comfort and joy.

As they played, Hannah's parents watched with fondness, their hearts swelling with gratitude for Destin's friendship. They knew how much Hannah cherished these moments, how they filled her with a sense of belonging she struggled to find elsewhere.

After a lively afternoon of play, the sun began to dip towards the horizon, casting a golden glow over the park. Reluctantly, Hannah and Destin made their way back to the picnic blanket, their cheeks flushed with exertion and laughter.

As they settled down to eat, Hannah's heart overflowed with gratitude for the friendship she had found in Destin. Despite the challenges she faced, moments like these reminded her that she was never alone—that there were people like Destin who saw beyond her differences and loved her just the same.

As they packed up their picnic and bid farewell to Destin, Hannah felt a sense of warmth settle over her. She knew that no matter what lay ahead, she would always have the love and support of friends like Destin, guiding her through life's adventures with joy and laughter.

Chapter 22: A Chance Encounter

Marcus, fulfilling the annual requirements of his offshore job, finds himself at the medical facility for his mandatory physical. As he waits in the bustling lobby, memories of the day Hannah was born flood his mind. It was a day filled with both joy and uncertainty, a defining moment in his life.

Amidst the movement of medical staff, Marcus notices a familiar face. Janay, a young nurse who had been present in the delivery room during Hannah's birth, catches his eye. The recognition sparks a connection to a significant moment in his past.

Approaching Janay with a warm smile, Marcus says, "Excuse me, are you nurse Edwards? I remember you from the day my child was born." Janay, initially surprised, smiles in acknowledgment as the memories of that day resurface.

They engage in a brief but heartfelt conversation, reminiscing about the emotions and events of that pivotal day. Janay, now a part of Marcus's memory associated with the birth of his daughter, shares a few kind words about how special that day was for her as well.

As Janay prepares to continue her duties, she departs with a smile, leaving Marcus reflecting on the passage of time. The chance encounter brings a sense of connection to the past, a reminder of the intricate web of lives intertwined in unexpected ways.

While Marcus acknowledges Janay's model figure, he is careful not to let his thoughts wander too far. His focus remains on the present moment and the responsibilities awaiting him. The encounter serves as a gentle reminder of the people who play fleeting yet meaningful roles in the chapters of our lives.

As Marcus completes his physical and prepares to return to his offshore job, he carries with him the warmth of the chance encounter. The chapter concludes with a sense of nostalgia and the realization that life is filled with unexpected connections, each person leaving a mark on the broader canvas of our experiences.

Chapter 23: A Night Unraveled

Layla, seeking solace and understanding, decides to go out with her friends to share her thoughts and concerns about the strain on her marriage and the challenges of raising Hannah. The night begins with a sense of anticipation, but little does Layla know that events at home will take an unexpected turn.

The chapter starts with Layla and her friends settling into a cozy corner of a restaurant. The ambiance is warm, and the low hum of conversation surrounds them as they order drinks and share appetizers. Layla, feeling a mixture of vulnerability and relief, opens up about the struggles she's been facing with Marcus and the growing impatience he seems to be displaying towards Hannah.

"I think that Marcus is getting burned out with Hannah. I think he's also embarrassed of her." Her friends, attentive and empathetic, offer words of comfort and advice. They listen intently as Layla shares her fears, frustrations, and the emotional toll it's taking on her. "Girrl, Marcus don't want us to "F" him up over you and Hannah. He don't want none of this." Layla laughs it off. The conversation becomes a therapeutic release for Layla, providing a sense of camaraderie and understanding.

Meanwhile, at home, Hannah is with a new babysitter Layla had arranged for the evening. The babysitter, however, calls Layla with unexpected news. She expresses concern about Hannah's behavior, explaining that she is acting out in a way that makes her uncomfortable continuing the care.

The news hits Layla like a sudden storm. The carefree atmosphere of the restaurant becomes suffocating as she receives the call. Bursting into tears, Layla informs her friends about the situation, feeling an immediate pull to be by her daughter's side.

The friends, supportive and caring, encourage Layla to go home and tend to Hannah. They assure her that they will understand and that there will be other moments to share and connect. Layla, feeling a mix of gratitude and desperation, quickly pays her part of the bill and rushes out of the restaurant.

The journey home is a blur for Layla as she grapples with a whirlwind of emotions. The once-anticipated night out with her girls has unraveled into a poignant reminder of the delicate balance she strives to maintain in her life.

Back at home, Layla finds Hannah upset and distressed. The babysitter, feeling overwhelmed, expresses her concerns, and Layla, despite her own emotional turmoil, thanks her for her honesty.

The chapter concludes with Layla holding Hannah close, her heart heavy with the challenges she faces. The unexpected turn of events becomes a catalyst for Layla to reassess the support system in place and seek solutions for the issues plaguing her marriage and family life. The night out, intended as an escape, instead becomes a catalyst for Layla's journey towards addressing the deeper issues within her family.

Chapter 24: Hannah's Checkup

As Layla and her mom accompany Hannah to her 12-year-old checkup, the routine appointment takes an unexpected turn. The doctor's office, a familiar yet often anxiety-inducing place for Hannah, becomes the setting for a conversation that navigates uncharted waters in her development.

As they wait for the doctor, Layla observes Hannah's unease, sensing that something is different this time. The nurse calls them in, and the trio enters the examination room. The doctor, a seasoned professional who has been overseeing Hannah's care for years, warmly greets them.

Dr. Sanchez, a kind-faced woman with years of experience, smiles warmly as they enter. "Hello, Hannah. Hello, Mrs. Evans. And how are we all doing today?" she asks, her tone gentle and reassuring.

During the examination, Layla, with a gentle touch, broaches the subject that has been on her mind. With a mix of concern and a mother's understanding, she discusses Hannah's recent onset of menstruation. The doctor, recognizing the challenges posed by Hannah's disability, engages in a compassionate dialogue.

"Layla, I understand this can be a difficult topic to discuss, especially given Hannah's unique needs," Dr. Sanchez begins, her voice calm and reassuring. "But I'm here to help in any way I can."

Hannah, sitting on the examination table, seems a bit apprehensive, her limited vocabulary and communication methods making it challenging for her to express herself fully. However, her use of the communication board becomes an essential means of conveying her needs.

Layla, in consultation with the doctor, discusses the option of using birth control to manage Hannah's menstrual cycle. The decision involves a delicate balance of medical considerations, Hannah's comfort, and the practicalities of her daily care. The doctor, aware of the unique challenges the family faces, offers guidance on the available options and their potential implications.

"I understand your concerns, Layla," Dr. Sanchez says, her tone empathetic. "We'll work together to find the best solution for Hannah."

The conversation extends beyond medical decisions, touching on the broader aspects of Hannah's growth and the ongoing journey of navigating life with a disability.

As the chapter unfolds, Layla grapples with the weight of making decisions on behalf of her daughter. The delicate dance of understanding Hannah's needs and ensuring her comfort becomes a poignant reminder of the complexities of parenting a child with a disability.

The chapter concludes with Layla leaving the doctor's office with Hannah, a sense of both responsibility and resilience guiding her. The journey into adolescence for a child with special needs poses unique challenges, and Layla, supported by her mother and the medical professionals, is determined to navigate these uncharted waters with love, care, and an unwavering commitment to Hannah's well-being.

Chapter 25: Feeling Burdened

The offshore wind whispered through the evening air as Marcus stepped off the boat, his two-week break from work officially beginning. Layla eagerly awaited his return, but as the days passed, she noticed that Marcus, though physically present, seemed emotionally distant at times. There were periods when he wasn't home, leaving Layla to wonder about the reasons behind his absence.

Concern crept into Layla's thoughts, and a mix of emotions brewed within her—was it infidelity, a reluctance to be burdened with family responsibilities, or perhaps a combination of both? The uncertainty gnawed at her, and she decided to address it with Marcus, seeking clarity on the situation.

Meanwhile, Marcus found solace in the familiar company of his friends, Billy and Tim, at a local bar. As they clinked glasses, Marcus opened up about the challenges he faced. "I think I'm starting to get burned out with my wife and daughter." Billy, the seasoned friend with a strong commitment to family, advised Marcus to stand by Layla and their daughter, emphasizing the importance of supporting them during tough times.

On the other hand, Tim took a different approach. In a moment of unexpected revelation, he shared that one of his acquaintances expressed interest in a more intimate relationship with Marcus. Shocked by Tim's disclosure, Marcus grappled with the conflicting advice from his friends.

The bar, filled with the ambient hum of conversations and clinking glasses, became a backdrop to Marcus's internal struggle. Now torn between the stability of his family life and the unexpected proposition presented by Tim's friend, Marcus had to navigate the complexities of his personal life.

As the night unfolded, Marcus faced pivotal decisions that would shape the dynamics of his relationship with Layla and the path his life would take in the upcoming weeks. The unresolved tension, coupled with the contrasting advice from Billy and Tim, left Marcus in a state of emotional turmoil, questioning the foundations of trust and commitment in his marriage.

As Marcus walked into the house after a tiring offshore stint, the aroma of his favorite meal greeted him. Layla, knowing his preferences, had meticulously prepared the dish. She had taken special care with her appearance, choosing shorts that accentuated her figure and slipping into one of Marcus' undershirts. The subtle allure was intentional, hoping to spend some intimate time with her husband after being apart for two weeks.

Hannah was peacefully asleep in her room, giving Layla the perfect opportunity to have some alone time with Marcus. However, as Layla observed her husband's reactions, she couldn't shake off the feeling that something was amiss. "What's wrong bae? Why are you unusually quiet? You know you can talk to me about anything." Marcus seemed distant, not displaying the usual affection he showered on her when he returned home.

Despite Layla's efforts to engage Marcus in conversation during dinner, he remained preoccupied, his mind seemingly elsewhere. The playful gestures and the tender moments they usually shared seemed to be missing. Layla felt a growing unease, a nagging suspicion that there might be something on Marcus's mind.

After dinner, Layla, sensing the emotional gap, decided to bridge it in a way she believed would strengthen their connection. She suggested an intimate moment between them, hoping to rekindle the spark that had seemingly dimmed during Marcus's absence. However, as they began to make love, Layla noticed a disconnect in Marcus's actions and demeanor.

It became apparent that Marcus's mind was wandering, focused on something or someone other than Layla. The physical intimacy that usually brought them closer seemed strained, leaving Layla feeling a sense of emptiness and confusion. She tried to draw Marcus into the present moment, searching for the connection they had shared before his departure.

The room, once filled with the scent of a home-cooked meal and the anticipation of reunion, now held an air of unspoken tension. Layla grappled with the sudden shift in dynamics, wondering if there was a hidden struggle or concern that Marcus was hesitant to share. As they lay side by side afterward, the silence hung heavy, and Layla couldn't shake the feeling that their relationship had entered a precarious phase, one that demanded honest communication and a resolution to the growing emotional distance.

Chapter 26: Tracey's Surprise

Layla is driving Hannah to school on a crisp morning. The sun is rising, casting a warm glow on the landscape. Hannah, nestled in her car seat, gazes out the window, her innocent eyes curious about the world around her. Layla, feeling the positive energy of the day, decides to turn on the radio.

As Layla scans through the stations, one of her favorite songs "Different" gospel songs starts playing. The melody fills the car, creating an uplifting atmosphere. Unable to resist the infectious beat, Layla's lips curl into a smile. She glances at Hannah in the rearview mirror, who seems equally intrigued by the music.

In a spontaneous burst of joy, Layla starts singing along with the song. Her voice, though not perfect, carries the enthusiasm of someone who simply enjoys the moment. To her surprise, Hannah's eyes light up, and a tiny smile graces her face. She notices that Hannah is desperately trying to sing along with her. "Difent" The mother-daughter duo finds themselves in an impromptu karaoke session, with Layla belting out the lyrics with joyful enthusiasm.

As Layla navigates through traffic, the car becomes a haven of shared happiness. The music not only connects Layla and Hannah but also serves as a bridge between generations, transcending any language barrier. Layla's heart swells with love for her daughter, grateful for these simple yet precious moments.

The song, a timeless melody that Layla has cherished for years, becomes a part of their shared memories. The car ride turns into more than just a commute; it transforms into a bonding experience, a small but significant chapter in the story of Layla and Hannah's relationship.

When they finally arrive at the school, Layla turns off the engine, but the music lingers in their hearts. She looks at Hannah and realizes that these fleeting moments of joy are the ones that define their connection. As Hannah steps out of the car, Layla can't help but feel grateful for the magic that music can create and the special bond they share, promising more musical adventures on their frequent car rides.

As Layla steps into the classroom alongside Hannah, her daughter's new teacher, Mrs. Tracey, greets her with an exciting revelation. Tracey beckons them over to a table, her face beaming with delight. Turning her attention to Hannah, Tracey requests, "Can you tell your mom your name?" Layla gazes at Hannah, her heart filled with anticipation.

"Haaanna Gaace Eeevans," Hannah utters. Though her speech may not be crystal clear, it resonates perfectly in Layla's ears. Overwhelmed with emotion, Layla's eyes well up, and tears cascade onto the classroom floor. Gratefully, she looks at Mrs. Tracey and expresses, "Thank you! Thank you for your incredible patience in teaching my precious child!"

In haste, Layla hurries back to her car to fetch her phone and share the exciting news about Hannah's progress with Marcus. She dials Marcus's number twice, but he doesn't answer, leaving Layla perplexed. "That's unlike him," she mutters. Eventually, Marcus returns her call, sounding somewhat breathless. "Hell-hello," he stammers. Layla explains she was calling to provide an update on their daughter's progress but notices he seems a bit preoccupied. Marcus admits he was on a morning jog and dropped his phone. Layla decides to save the good news for dinner instead.

Chapter 27: Unveiling Secrets

As the anticipation for Marcus's arrival grows, Layla, her mother Mary, and Hannah sit at the dining room table with dinner slowly getting cold. They had planned to surprise Marcus with the news of Hannah's progress, but he hasn't shown up yet. Mary, observing Layla's concern, leans in and expresses her suspicions about Marcus, wondering if he might be cheating or avoiding the responsibilities of fatherhood.

Intrigued by the idea, Mary suggests that Layla should discreetly check Marcus's phone while he's asleep to uncover any potential clues. Layla hesitates, torn between trusting her husband and wanting to address the uncertainties Mary has brought to light. The atmosphere in the room becomes tense as they wait for Marcus and grapple with the uncertainty of his delayed arrival.

Layla, feeling a mixture of disappointment and frustration, tries to compose herself as Marcus returns home late. Her initial excitement to share the news of Hannah's progress is overshadowed by the tension in the air. Marcus attempts to speak to Layla, but her upset state prevents her from sharing the positive news.

Meanwhile, Marcus, sensing Layla's distress, decides to seek advice from Ms. Mary, who remains unusually silent and unresponsive. After seeing her mother out, Layla, feeling overwhelmed, retreats to the bathroom and vents her emotions by slamming the door. Determined to find solace, she draws a bath, turns on soothing gospel music, and submerges herself to unwind and relax.

As Layla emerges from the bath, hoping for a peaceful resolution, she discovers Marcus lying across the bed, fast asleep. His phone, innocently resting on the nightstand, becomes a source of temptation for Layla. Unable to resist the urge, she grabs the phone and hastily returns to the bathroom to unlock it and read his messages.

To Layla's dismay, she finds messages and pictures exchanged between Marcus and another woman – a young lady seemingly in her late twenties. The discovery sends shockwaves through Layla, leaving her grappling with a mix of emotions and the sudden revelation of potential infidelity. The atmosphere in the room becomes charged with the weight of unspoken truths and the uncertainty of what lies ahead.

Layla entered one of the other bedrooms in the house and collapsed onto the bed. Tears welled up as she cried out into the pillow. Despite her intense emotions, Layla had devised a plan to confront Marcus, but she needed more information before executing it. "I need to maintain composure and not reveal that I'm onto him just yet," she resolved.

Struggling with her usual sleep difficulties, Layla opened the cabinet and reached for her sleeping medication. As she held the bottle of pills, she gazed at it momentarily, eventually extracting only one pill. "What was I thinking? I need to regain control of myself."

Layla woke up with a heavy heart, grappling with the unsettling discovery of messages on Marcus's phone. However, she decided she wasn't quite ready to confront him about it just yet. The tension between them was palpable, and Layla was determined to focus on her responsibilities for the day.

With Hannah's dentist appointment at "Boss Family Dentistry" looming, Layla took charge, despite the usual routine of having Marcus by her side to assist. When Marcus tentatively offered his company, saying, "You want me to come with you, bae?" Layla remained silent, refusing to his presence.

Heading into Hannah's room, Layla completed the task of dressing her daughter while pointedly ignoring Marcus, enveloping him in a heavy blanket of silence. Layla led Hannah to the car, efficiently securing her in the seat belt before slamming the car door shut. With a determined expression, Layla sped away, leaving Marcus standing there, bewildered and searching for answers in the rearview mirror. The air hung thick with unspoken tension as Layla drove away, the weight of her emotions steering the course of her actions for the moment.

Chapter 28: Turbulent Tides

As Layla's car rolled to a stop in the dentist's parking lot, the unease inside the vehicle was palpable. The absence of her husband, Marcus, was a stark reminder of the strain their relationship had been under lately. Layla took a deep breath, steeling herself for what awaited inside the dental office.

Hannah, had been surprisingly calm during the car ride. The air inside the vehicle seemed thick with tension, though, hinting at the storm brewing beneath the surface. As they approached the dentist's office, something changed. Hannah's eyes widened, and a sudden anxiety gripped her.

Layla glanced at her daughter, concern etched across her face. "Hannah, sweetie, we're here. Everything will be fine," Layla reassured, but her words seemed to fall on deaf ears.

As Hannah caught sight of the dentist's office building, her composure shattered. She began to act out, a mix of fear and discomfort evident in her actions. Layla, struggling with her daughter, felt the weight of the stares from other patients in the parking lot. She was upset, agitated, and a little embarrassed by the scene unfolding.

Just as Layla was reaching her limit, two compassionate dental assistants emerged from the office. Offering a helping hand, they could sense Layla's distress. Grateful, Layla accepted their assistance, though she ultimately decided it was best to take Hannah back home.

The drive back was a mix of tears and conflicted thoughts for Layla. The tension between her and Marcus was like a heavy fog, hanging in the air. In addition to the challenges with Hannah, Layla couldn't escape the nagging suspicion of possible infidelity on Marcus's part.

Seeking solace, Layla dialed her mother's number. The voice on the other end of the line provided comfort through prayer and encouraging words. Despite the support, Layla couldn't shake the turmoil inside her.

Arriving home, Layla's emotions reached a breaking point when she spotted Marcus outside. Without giving him a chance to explain, Layla erupted. "Get Hannah!" she yelled, her frustration pouring out. Marcus, wearing a confused expression, hurriedly complied, bringing Hannah into the house.

Attempting to address Layla's pain, Marcus approached her on the living room couch. He tried to speak, but Layla, consumed by her emotions, couldn't bear to hear him out. She screamed at him to go away, the weight of her feelings and the day's events pushing her to the edge. The door slammed shut, leaving Marcus standing in the silence, unsure of how to mend the fractures that had deepened within their family.

Chapter 29: Uncharted Waters

After the heated exchange with Layla, Marcus stormed out of the house, his emotions in disarray. Determined to find an escape, he decided to head to the bar and join his friends, Billy and Tim.

As Marcus settled into a dimly lit corner of the bar, nursing his drink and lost in his own thoughts, a young lady caught his eye. She had an air of confidence and beauty that was hard to ignore – flawless skin, hazel eyes that seemed to hold a story, and a physique that hinted at dedication to the gym.

Trying not to be obvious, Marcus attempted to avert his gaze, but the allure of the mysterious woman was too strong. Sensing his troubled demeanor, she took the initiative to strike up a conversation. "Bad day?" she asked, her voice a soft melody in the noisy bar.

Marcus, with his head still down, initially ignored her, lost in his own world. "Where is Tim and Billy?" he muttered to himself, more as a rhetorical question than seeking an answer.

Undeterred, the lady reached out, running her hand down Marcus' arm, a gesture that caught his attention. "You work out too?" she inquired, her eyes tracing the contours of his masculinity.

He finally lifted his head, the alcohol beginning to dull the edges of his frustration. "I was just born this way," Marcus replied with a hint of humor, trying to lighten the mood. The two found themselves engaged in conversation, sharing stories and laughter, their drinks gradually turning into a shared escape from the complexities waiting for them outside the bar.

An hour passed, and the bar's atmosphere became a blur as Marcus and the lady continued to lose themselves in conversation and the numbing effects of alcohol. Eventually, they decided to leave, stepping out into the night, oblivious to the world around them.

Coincidentally, as they exited one door, Billy and Tim entered through another. The surprise on their faces was evident as they exchanged nudges, glancing at Marcus with a mix of shock and curiosity. The uncharted waters of Marcus's evening had taken an unexpected turn, leaving questions hanging in the air as the four individuals crossed paths in the doorway of the dimly lit bar.

Chapter 30: Unraveling Secrets

Marcus and the young lady stumbled out of the dimly lit bar, laughter and alcohol fogging their senses. The world spun around them as they hailed a cab, their unsteady steps a testament to the intoxication that engulfed them. In their inebriated state, they made the impulsive decision to escape the city lights and venture to a hotel on the outskirts.

The cab ride was a blur, the driver navigating through the night as Marcus and the young lady exchanged drunken banter. Eventually, they arrived at a quiet hotel, checked in, and stumbled into a room that would become the setting for a night of regret.

Morning sunlight pierced through the curtains, waking Marcus with a pounding headache and a gnawing sense of remorse. As he held his head in his hands, he turned to see the lady beside him – a face he didn't fully recognize in the sober light of day.

Confusion clouded Marcus' stare as he grappled with the remnants of a hazy night. It was only when he spoke that the pieces fell into place. "What have I done?" he uttered, looking at the woman beside him. It was a question that lingered in the air, unanswered.

As Marcus tried to make sense of the situation, his phone erupted with missed calls and messages from Layla. Panic set in as he realized the magnitude of the mistake he had made. Apologizing profusely to Elaine, whose name he just learned, Marcus explained the circumstances – the alcohol, the vulnerability, the shared culpability.

Elaine, though taken aback, reassured Marcus. "Don't be too hard on yourself," she said, her own guilt evident. "We both made mistakes."

In that moment, Marcus discovered a shocking revelation – Elaine was actually Layla's best friend's sister. The weight of his actions became even more pronounced, intertwining his personal life with a connection that carried unexpected layers of complexity and emotion.

As Marcus and Elaine grappled with the aftermath, unaware of the eyes that had witnessed their departure, they pledged to keep their indiscretion a secret. Little did they know that Tim and Billy, friends who had observed them leaving the bar, were now harboring suspicions. Layla, Marcus' wife, also had an inkling that something was amiss.

The unfolding drama, a tapestry of secrets and lies, would test the bonds of trust and loyalty, threatening to unravel the delicate threads that held Marcus' life together.

Chapter 31: Unveiling Betrayal

The clock struck 3 a.m. as Marcus stumbled towards his home, his steps heavy with the weight of guilt and the lingering scent of alcohol and a night of indiscretion. The dimly lit street seemed to magnify the shadows that danced on his conscience.

Silently unlocking the door, Marcus tiptoed into the house, hoping to evade Layla's notice. The challenge, however, lay in concealing the evidence embedded in his clothing – the unmistakable aroma of a one-night stand. Anxiety fueled his haste as he hurried towards the downstairs bathroom, his only refuge for a quick, guilt-ridden shower.

Aware of the risk of entering the master bedroom, Marcus opted for a different strategy. The house boasted 2 1/2 bathrooms, and he chose the one downstairs, intending to emerge looking as though he had been there all along. Little did he remember the nanny cam discreetly watching over Hannah's room.

In his intoxicated stupor, Marcus had overlooked the consequences of his actions. Layla, now awake, witnessed every move on the nanny cam. A mix of hurt and anger colored her voice as she muttered, "Stupid ass." She made a silent decision not to confront Marcus until after she took Hannah to school.

Layla's alarm, set for 6 a.m. on weekdays, shattered the uneasy silence, signaling the beginning of a day destined for confrontation. Without going back to sleep after the shocking revelation on the nanny cam, Layla proceeded to Hannah's room. Tears silently streamed down her cheeks as she carefully took Hannah out of the room, determined not to disturb Marcus.

The ride to Hannah's special needs school felt endless, the weight of impending confrontation hanging heavy in the air. The familiar strains of gospel music, their solace in times of trouble, played softly in the background. The local gospel rap artist's "Pray for Me" resonated, usually a source of comfort for Layla. However, this time, her mind was solely focused on the confrontation awaiting her at home.

As Layla dropped Hannah off at school, the tears she had held back flowed freely. The journey back home seemed longer than ever, the gospel station providing a bittersweet soundtrack to her thoughts. The lyrics of prayer and solace could not mask the determination building within Layla – a resolve to confront Marcus and face the painful reality of his betrayal.

Chapter 32: Confronting Reality

As Layla stepped into their home, a mix of exhaustion and determination etched on her face, she was greeted by the unmistakable sounds of Marcus retching in their master bathroom. The stench of alcohol permeated the air, and Layla's question about his well-being carried more indifference than genuine concern.

"You okay, bae?" she asked, her tone betraying a lack of genuine interest. Her focus shifted immediately to the matter at hand – where Marcus had been the previous night.

Marcus, still nursing the remnants of a hangover, glanced at Layla with a feigned innocence, as if oblivious to her inquiry. "I spent the night in Hannah's room," he claimed, offering an excuse that seemed feeble even to his own ears. Layla's skepticism was palpable.

"Oh really," Layla responded dryly, her disbelief evident. Unfazed by his attempts at deception, she confronted him with the truth. Layla had called him repeatedly, sent text messages – attempts to reach him that went unanswered. Her eyes, filled with a mix of hurt and anger, met Marcus's gaze as she revealed the damning evidence she had witnessed on the nanny cam in Hannah's room.

While interrogating him with the intensity of a prosecutor, Layla began bagging up Marcus's clothing, a symbolic act of severing ties. She made it clear that she refused to tolerate cheating and lies. "Get your shit and go," she demanded, her voice resolute.

The realization of the impending breakup hit Marcus, but Layla remained steadfast. She knew that raising a disabled child alone would be challenging, but the thought of being with a husband she could no longer trust was more unbearable. Layla couldn't risk ending up in a domestic violence situation that might jeopardize Hannah's well-being and their bond.

Determined to uphold her strength and protect her daughter, Layla reached out to her mom for support. Her mother, outraged by Marcus's actions, was ready to confront him herself. Layla, however, sought to keep the situation under control, not wanting Hannah to sense the turmoil brewing within their home. In the midst of the emotional storm, Layla navigated the difficult path of separation, fueled by a fierce determination to shield her daughter from the fallout of betrayal.

Chapter 33: Shattered Trust

The night was heavy with the weight of Layla's heartache, and her tears seemed to be an unending river of sorrow. The decision to put Marcus out of their home, the home they had built together, weighed on her like an anchor pulling her down into a sea of despair. Layla's mother, Mary, sensing the gravity of her daughter's pain, stayed the night by her side.

Mary had taken over the care of Hannah, as Layla was in no state to attend to her. Layla's sobs echoed through the house, each cry a testament to the betrayal she had experienced. Mary tried her best to console her daughter, offering words of comfort and understanding, but the wound was fresh, and Layla's pain was palpable.

In the midst of Layla's anguish, she reached out to her closest friends, Fee and Tori, a circle of confidantes who had been there through thick and thin. As Layla poured out her heart, sharing the painful truth about Marcus's infidelity, her friends rallied around her. The anger and disbelief in their voices mirrored Layla's own emotions, and they vowed to confront Marcus.

Meanwhile, Marcus, desperate to salvage what was left of his marriage, reached out to his buddies, Billy and Tim. He tried to plead his case, explaining the situation from his perspective. However, his attempts to justify his actions faltered when Tim revealed that he had seen Marcus leaving the bar with the woman with whom he had cheated on Layla.

Billy, a loyal friend who recognized the gravity of the situation, advised Marcus to do whatever it took to make amends with his wife. On the other hand, Tim, with a tone of sarcastic humor, remarked, "I hope it was good." It was clear that Marcus's actions had consequences not only on his marriage but also on the friendships he held dear.

Undeterred, Marcus continued to call Layla, hoping for a chance to explain himself and seek forgiveness. However, Layla, still grappling with the betrayal, refused to answer his calls. The one time Marcus managed to get through, it was Mary who picked up the phone, delivering a barrage of profanity before abruptly hanging up on him.

Feeling the weight of Layla's silence, Marcus reluctantly decided to give her space, hoping that time and distance might allow wounds to heal. It was a painful realization that the consequences of his actions were irreparable.

Layla decided to confide in two of her other close friends who had just come home for a visit. Layla's friends, sensing her pain and vulnerability, gathered around her with open arms and compassionate hearts. They listened attentively as Layla poured out her anguish and confusion, recounting the painful details of Marcus's betrayal.

"I just don't understand how he could do this to me," Layla whispered, her voice trembling with emotion. "We were supposed to be a team, partners in life. How could he throw it all away for someone else?"

Her friend Keisha reached out and squeezed Layla's hand gently. "I know it's hard to make sense of it all right now, but you are not alone in this. We are here for you, no matter what."

Another friend, Niki, nodded in agreement. "You are stronger than you realize, Layla. This is just a temporary setback, and you will come out of it even stronger. You deserve someone who respects and cherishes you, not someone who betrays your trust."

Tears welled up in Layla's eyes as she felt the warmth and support of her friends enveloping her. "Thank you," she whispered hoarsely. "I don't know what I would do without you all."

As the evening wore on, Layla found comfort in the laughter and camaraderie of her friends, grateful for their unwavering love and support during her darkest hours. Together, they vowed to stand by each other through thick and thin, united in their journey towards healing and redemption

Chapter 34: Coping with Change

As Marcus settled into his parents' home, he clung to the hope that Layla would eventually cool off, that time apart would pave the way for forgiveness, and he could return home to Layla and Hannah. However, Layla, devastated by the betrayal, found herself caught in a storm of conflicting emotions. Her mother and best friends, having witnessed her pain, strongly discouraged her from allowing Marcus back into their lives.

Despite the emotional turmoil, Layla was determined to navigate the challenges of raising Hannah, their special needs daughter, on her own. The weight of responsibility grew heavier with each passing day, and Layla faced the daily struggle of dressing Hannah and ensuring she made it to school on time. At now, sixteen, Hannah's behavior had become increasingly combative, both at school and at home.

The changes in Hannah's life seemed to exacerbate her challenges. A new teacher had entered the picture at her special needs school, and Hannah resisted the alterations with a newfound intensity. The teacher, lacking the patience required for working with special needs students, struggled to connect with Hannah. The situation escalated when Hannah, overwhelmed and frustrated, resorted to biting both the teacher and several classmates.

Layla sat across from the principal and Hannah's teacher, her heart heavy with concern and worry. The principal, Mrs. Stepney, spoke first, her tone gentle yet firm.

"Layla, we wanted to meet with you to discuss Hannah's recent behavior at school," Mrs. Stepney began, her expression empathetic. "We've noticed some concerning patterns, including frequent outbursts, difficulty with transitions, and a decline in engagement."

Layla's heart sank as she listened, her mind racing with thoughts of Hannah's well-being. "I had no idea things had gotten this challenging," she admitted, her voice barely above a whisper.

Hannah's teacher, Mrs. Doris, nodded in understanding. "It's clear that Hannah is struggling, especially given her recent diagnosis and the changes at home," she explained gently. "We believe that her autism and the absence of her father may be contributing to her behavior."

Tears welled up in Layla's eyes as she absorbed the weight of their words. "I've been trying my best to support her, but I didn't realize how much she was struggling," she confessed, her voice breaking. "I feel like I've failed her."

Mrs. Doris reached out and placed a comforting hand on Layla's shoulder. "You're not alone in this, Layla," she assured her. "We're here to support you and Hannah every step of the way."

Layla nodded, grateful for their understanding and support. "Thank you," she whispered, her voice filled with emotion. "I'll do whatever it takes to help Hannah through this."

As the meeting continued, Layla and the school staff brainstormed strategies to support Hannah's unique needs both academically and emotionally. Together, they formed a plan to provide her with the specialized resources and support she needed to thrive despite the challenges she faced at home. And as Layla left the meeting, she felt a glimmer of hope amidst the darkness, knowing that she and Hannah were not alone in their journey.

It was a heartbreaking realization, but Layla, determined to prioritize Hannah's well-being, made a difficult decision. She decided to homeschool Hannah, believing that the familiar and controlled environment at home would provide the stability Hannah needed. Layla understood that this new challenge would demand more of her time and energy, but her commitment to her daughter's safety and emotional well-being took precedence.

The decision to homeschool was not made lightly, and Layla sought the support of therapists and specialists to tailor an education plan suited to Hannah's unique needs. It marked the beginning of a new chapter for Layla and Hannah, a chapter defined by resilience, sacrifice, and a mother's unwavering love.

As Layla navigated the uncharted territory of homeschooling, she held onto the hope that, in time, both she and Hannah would find healing and stability. The journey ahead was uncertain, but Layla faced it with determination, refusing to let the challenges define their future.

Chapter 35: A New Beginning

As Layla embarked on her journey of homeschooling Hannah, she made significant adjustments to her own life. Taking a new job with a flexible schedule allowed her to spend more time with her daughter. The decision to hire a special needs homeschool teacher, Ms. Karen, marked a turning point in their lives.

On the day of Ms. Karen's first visit, Layla felt a mixture of anxiety and hope. "You can go ahead to work, Mrs. Evans; Hannah is in good hands with me," reassured Ms. Karen. Reluctantly, Layla left the comfort of her home, heading to her job where she assisted low-income elderly citizens with daily tasks.

Throughout the day, Layla checked the hidden nanny cam from time to time, finding solace in seeing Hannah interacting positively with her new teacher. The flexibility of her job allowed

Layla to balance work and her commitment to Hannah, even though the challenges of raising a special needs child persisted.

Amidst the routines of her workday, Layla's phone rang persistently. Marcus's name flashed on the screen, a reminder of the past that Layla desperately wanted to leave behind. Ignoring the calls twice, Layla eventually answered the third time, her voice sharp with frustration.

"Why the hell are you calling me?" Layla demanded. "Shouldn't you be calling the bitch you cheated with?"

Marcus stumbled over his words, attempting to explain himself, but Layla had heard enough. "If you're calling to ask about Hannah, she's now being homeschooled. She's adjusted to her daddy not being around. You lacked patience with our daughter also. Maybe in the future, I can co-parent with you, but right now, I hate your cheating ass guts."

Hanging up the phone, Layla felt a mixture of relief and anger. The weight of her emotions pressed upon her, and she realized that harboring hatred towards Marcus would only consume her. In a moment of introspection, Layla decided she needed to pray and seek God's forgiveness.

"I need to ask for forgiveness for my hatred of Marcus," Layla admitted to herself. "Hate is only going to consume me." With determination, she set aside time for prayer, seeking the strength to let go of the anger and resentment that threatened to overshadow the new beginning she was trying to build for herself and Hannah.

As Layla navigated the complexities of work, homeschooling, and the emotional turmoil of her personal life, she held onto the hope that this new chapter would bring healing, growth, and a brighter future for both her and Hannah. The journey was far from easy, but Layla's resilience and love for her daughter guided her through each challenge.

Chapter 36: The Weight of Decisions

As Layla grapples with the growing challenges of caring for Hannah on her own, she leans heavily on the support of her mother and friends. Their unwavering presence offers her solace and strength during moments of uncertainty. Yet, despite their support, Layla finds herself facing one of the most agonizing decisions of her life – whether to place Hannah in an assisted living program.

The thought of separating from Hannah, even if it's for her own well-being, tears at Layla's heart. She spends sleepless nights wrestling with the decision, torn between her desire to provide the best care for Hannah and the fear of losing the precious bond they share. " I feel like I'm failing you, Hannah." Seeking guidance, Layla turns to prayer, pouring out her heart to God and begging for clarity and peace in her decision-making.

In her moments of vulnerability, Layla reaches out to Marcus, hoping for his support and understanding. However, his new girlfriend intercepts Layla's attempts at communication, deleting her calls and text messages. " I can't believe he's not answering my calls." The rejection wounds Layla deeply, yet she refuses to let it deter her from doing what's best for Hannah.

Taking a leave of absence from her job, Layla commits herself fully to caring for Hannah, determined to avoid the prospect of assisted living for as long as possible. But as the demands of caregiving weigh heavily on her shoulders, Layla begins to feel the strain of isolation and loneliness.

In an attempt to reclaim a semblance of normalcy in her life, Layla tentatively dips her toes into the world of dating. However, the reality of her situation soon becomes apparent when she realizes she can't leave Hannah for extended periods of time. Instead of venturing out on the town, Layla invites her date over for a romantic dinner at her home.

The doorbell rings and Layla goes to the door. "Glad you decided to show up." It was a friend of hers that she had been knowing since high school, Patrick. The evening starts off promisingly, and she and Patrick were really enjoying their night and getting reacquainted. It was definitely something Layla needed, someone who could show her a good time and distract her from everything she has been dealing with since her separation with Marcus. Patrick and Layla had just finished their candle light dinner and headed to the couch to watch a movie. Hannah enters the room where her mom and Patrick were sitting. Hannah reacts negatively to the presence of a stranger in their home. "Introduce me to this beautiful little lady." "This is my daughter, Hannah Grace." Hannah lets out a scream and charges toward Patrick. She rips his designer shirt! "What the fuck is wrong with her?" he asks angrily. Layla's hopes for a successful date quickly unravel. As the night ends with Patrick storming out the door and speeding off in his car, Layla is left grappling with the realization that she may never find companionship and that her responsibilities as a mother to Hannah will always come first, even if it means sacrificing her own happiness.

In the midst of uncertainty and heartache, Layla clings to the hope that God will provide her with the strength and wisdom she needs to navigate the challenges ahead. With faith as her anchor, Layla continues to press forward, determined to make the best decisions for herself and, above all, for the precious daughter who has captured her heart.

Chapter 37: Family Ties and Difficult Conversations

Layla's heart weighs heavy with worry as she leaves Hannah in the capable hands of Ms. Karen, their special needs home school teacher, in order to seek out Marcus at his parents' house. Despite the turmoil in her own relationship with Marcus, Layla finds solace in the familiar embrace of his family, particularly his mother, Ms. Danita.

Ms. Danita welcomes Layla with open arms, her warm smile a reminder of the bond they share as family. As Layla pours out her concerns about Hannah's escalating issues and her struggles to reach Marcus, Ms. Danita listens with a compassionate ear, offering words of reassurance and support.

"I will make sure Marcus knows about your attempts to reach him," Ms. Danita promises, her maternal instincts kicking in. "No matter what you and Marcus are going through, you will always be family to us."

However, Layla's mention of the possibility of placing Hannah in an assisted living facility strikes a nerve with Ms. Danita. The thought of her granddaughter being cared for by strangers, no matter how well-equipped they may be, fills her with apprehension and sadness.

"I can't bear the thought of Hannah being cared for by anyone other than family," Ms. Danita confesses, her voice trembling with emotion. "She deserves to be surrounded by love and familiarity, not strangers."

Despite her own disappointment and frustration, Layla understands Ms. Danita's perspective. The bond between family members runs deep, and the idea of entrusting Hannah's care to outsiders is a difficult pill to swallow for both of them.

As Layla waits anxiously for Marcus to arrive, hoping for a chance to talk to him face to face, she can't shake the feeling of disappointment when he fails to show up. Unbeknownst to Layla, Marcus's girlfriend's timely intervention has diverted his attention elsewhere, leaving Layla feeling abandoned and alone once again.

With a heavy heart, Layla bids farewell to Marcus's parents, her mind filled with unresolved questions and concerns about Hannah's future. As she drives away from the familiar comfort of Marcus's childhood home, Layla can't help but wonder if she'll ever find the answers she so desperately seeks, or if she'll be forced to make the painful decision about Hannah's care on her own.

Chapter Title 38: The Weight of Responsibility

Layla's heart felt heavy as she left Marcus' parent's home, her mind swirling with a torrent of emotions. The betrayal of her husband, the uncertainty of her daughter's future, and the overwhelming burden of caring for Hannah alone weighed on her shoulders like a leaden cloak. The Gospel song, "Thank You," played softly in the background, a faint attempt to soothe her fractured spirit, but even its comforting melodies couldn't drown out the cacophony of her thoughts.

Lost in her own turmoil, Layla drove on autopilot, her hands gripping the steering wheel with a mechanical detachment. She ignored the incessant buzzing of her phone, the caller ID flashing with the name of her concerned cousin, Debbie. She couldn't bear to confront the questions, the sympathy, the pity that awaited her on the other end of the line.

Unfocused and preoccupied, Layla's attention slipped as she navigated through the familiar neighborhood streets. The sudden jolt of the car hitting a speed hump snapped her back to reality, her heart pounding in her chest. For a moment, panic threatened to overwhelm her, but she clenched her teeth and forced herself to take a deep breath.

"Let me get ahold of myself," she muttered under her breath, her voice barely audible over the hum of the engine. "There are plenty of single mothers who have children with disabilities. I can do this."

With a shaky resolve, Layla pressed on, the image of her daughter's smiling face flashing in her mind's eye. She had to be strong for Hannah, no matter what challenges lay ahead.

Pulling into the garage, Layla's ears were assaulted by the frantic cries of Hannah's sitter. Without hesitation, she flung open the car door and sprinted towards the house, her heart hammering in her chest. Dread coiled in the pit of her stomach, a cold knot of fear tightening with every step.

As Layla burst through the front door, her worst fears were realized in a scene of chaos and confusion. The sitter stood in the living room, her face a mask of horror as she gazed upon the scene before her. Hannah lay motionless on the floor, her tiny body twisted in an unnatural angle, her cries piercing the air like a dagger to Layla's heart.

Time seemed to stand still as Layla rushed to her daughter's side, her hands trembling as she cradled Hannah in her arms. Tears streamed down her cheeks as she whispered words of comfort, her voice choked with emotion.

Nothing could have prepared Layla for the gut-wrenching agony of seeing her precious daughter in pain. But in that moment of despair, she found a strength she never knew she possessed – a fierce determination to protect and care for her child, no matter the cost.

And as she held Hannah close, rocking her gently in her arms, Layla knew that she would do whatever it took to give her daughter the love and support she needed to thrive, even in the face of overwhelming adversity

Chapter 39: Crisis Strikes

As Layla's heart pounded in her chest, panic surged through her veins. Hannah lay on the floor unconscious and her body convulsing. Layla's voice cut through the chaos, instructing the sitter to dial for an ambulance while she knelt beside Hannah, her hands trembling as she tried to soothe her daughter.

"Hannah, stay with me," she whispered, her voice thick with emotion. "Just keep breathing, sweetheart. Help is on the way."

But as they waited, time seemed to stretch infinitely, each second an eternity of uncertainty. Desperation gripped Layla's soul, and in a moment of instinctive faith, she began to pray. Her voice quivered with emotion as she whispered words of comfort and hope, her fingers intertwined with Hannah's.

And then, as if a lifeline had been thrown from the heavens, Layla remembered Hannah's favorite song. With a voice raw with emotion, she sang, pouring every ounce of love and strength into the melody until the ambulance's wail pierced through the air.

Paramedics swarmed around them, their practiced movements a blur of efficiency as they tended to Hannah. In the midst of the commotion, Layla's trembling fingers fumbled for her phone, her heart sinking as Marcus's number rang unanswered.

Frantic, she dialed Marcus's mother, her words rushed and urgent as she relayed the situation. But when she mentioned Marcus's silence, his mother's sharp retort cut through the tension.

"I know that boy ain't blocking your calls," she exclaimed. "Let me hang up and call him from my phone." After speaking with Marcus and scolding him in the process, Marcus hangs up with his mom and calls Layla.

With a sense of dread gnawing at her, Layla watched as Marcus's name flashed on the screen, her heart pounding in her chest as he finally calls.

"Marcus, where are you?" Layla's voice cracked with emotion. "Hannah needs you."

But Marcus's confusion mirrored her own as he sifted through his missed calls and messages, realization dawning in his eyes.

Looking towards his girlfriend Janice, he asks, "You blocked my wife's calls, didn't you?" His accusation hung heavy in the air, his anger palpable.

Before Janice could respond, Marcus stormed off to his truck and drove viciously to the emergency room, his mind consumed with worry for his daughter. With hazard lights flashing, he navigated the streets, each passing moment fueling his determination.

Inside the hospital, Layla paced the sterile halls, her heart heavy with uncertainty. When Marcus finally arrived, tension crackled between them, but in that moment, all that mattered was Hannah.

"I didn't think you were coming," Layla admitted, her voice trembling with emotion.

Marcus's gaze softened, the weight of his words heavy with regret. "I won't let anyone else come between me and my family." "Not anymore," he vowed, his hand reaching for hers. "Not ever."

Chapter 40: A Uniting Prayer

Layla and Marcus sat in the sterile waiting room of the hospital, their nerves frayed and hearts heavy with worry for their daughter, Hannah. Despite the tension that often lingered between them, their shared concern for their child bridged the gap that divided them. They clasped each other's hands tightly, finding solace in their connection as they awaited the news.

As minutes stretched into what felt like hours, the silence between them was broken only by the occasional sniffle or whispered prayer. Tears streaked down their cheeks, a testament to the depth of their fear and the intensity of their hope.

"Sometimes good things can come out of bad situations," Layla murmured, her voice soft but resolute in the face of uncertainty. Marcus nodded in agreement, his own voice choked with emotion as he echoed her sentiment.

Their moment of shared vulnerability was interrupted by the arrival of the doctor, whose presence loomed large in the cramped space of the emergency room. With a heavy heart, he delivered the news they had been dreading: Hannah had suffered a seizure. Though the diagnosis was dire, there was a glimmer of hope in the doctor's reassurance that she would be under observation overnight and could potentially go home the next day.

"Take care of your precious daughter," the doctor urged, his words a solemn reminder of the fragility of life and the importance of cherishing every moment.

The following day brought a sense of relief as Hannah was discharged from the hospital, her parents breathing a collective sigh of gratitude as they prepared to return home. Yet, amidst the joy of their daughter's recovery, tensions simmered just beneath the surface, threatening to resurface the moment they stepped foot in familiar surroundings.

As they crossed the threshold of their home, they were met with the sight of Layla's mother, Mary, her expression a mixture of concern and consternation. Marcus brushed past her without a word, his focus squarely on Hannah as he carried her into the sanctuary of her bedroom.

"Come here, Layla," Mary called out, her voice tinged with a hint of reproach. Layla bristled at the sound, her patience worn thin by the events of the past few days.

"I don't have time for your shit right now, Mama," Layla snapped, her frustration bubbling to the surface. Mary raised an eyebrow at her daughter's outburst, a knowing look passing between them as she spoke.

"I know you ain't letting his cheating ass get off this easily. But I'm gonna let this go for now, until Hannah gets better," Mary conceded, her words a silent acknowledgment of the delicate balance they were all struggling to maintain.

With Hannah's health hanging in the balance, Layla and Marcus were forced to set aside their differences and come together in their shared love for their daughter. And as they navigated the uncertain road ahead, they found strength in the bonds of family and the power of prayer to guide them through even the darkest of times.

Chapter 41: Finding the Right Care

As Layla and Marcus sat down to discuss their plans for hiring a permanent in-home sitter for Hannah, they knew they needed someone special. With Marcus' decision to return to work full-time, finding the right caregiver became a top priority. They wanted someone who not only had experience but also specialized in working with individuals with disabilities.

After scouring through listings and recommendations, they set up interviews to find the perfect fit. It was crucial for them to find someone who could understand and cater to Hannah's needs. After several rounds of interviews, they finally found someone who seemed promising – Lexi.

Lexi came with over 15 years of experience in assisting individuals with disabilities. Her demeanor during the interview showed patience, care, and genuine compassion. Layla and Marcus felt a sense of relief knowing that Hannah would be in good hands.

On Lexi's first day with Hannah, Marcus couldn't help but commend her on her demeanor. "You're great with her," he exclaimed, feeling reassured as he left for work. Before departing, Marcus ensured that Lexi had all the necessary information and reassured her to make herself at home while taking care of their princess.

Throughout the day, Lexi engaged with Hannah, showing patience and understanding as she played with sensory toys, colored in her favorite book, and watched her beloved TV show. Layla observed Lexi's interactions with Hannah and felt a sense of gratitude knowing that they had found someone who truly cared for their daughter's well-being.

After feeling comfortable with Lexi, Layla finally decides to leave and run a few errands. Feeling a weight lift off her shoulders after Layla's departure, Lexi lounged on the living room couch. Since Hannah was asleep, Layla took a moment to chat with her boyfriend, who worked nearby. "This is my kind of job," she remarked, feeling content in her role.

As the day passed, Layla and Marcus returned home to find Hannah content and well-cared for, reaffirming their decision to hire Lexi. With Lexi's compassionate care, they felt confident in balancing their work commitments while ensuring Hannah's happiness and safety.

Chapter 42: Inquisitive Interrogation

Mary's visit to Layla's home the next day was never a subtle affair. Her southern accent carried her questions like a melody, but her curiosity often bordered on intrusion. As she settled into Layla's living room, her eyes fell on Lexi, the new in-home care provider.

"Where you from, and who ya people?" Mary's inquiry cut through the air, as if she were sizing Lexi up with her words.

Lexi, with a slight frown, responded evenly, "I'm from Texas, but I moved back here to be closer to family."

Mary persisted, undeterred. "How long have you been working with the disabled?"

Lexi's patience wore thin, but she maintained her composure. "I hope that I don't come off as being rude, but I've already gone through the interview process with Mr. and Mrs. Evans. I understand your concerns, but I'm quite sure they can tell you all about me."

Mary's lips pursed in a knowing manner. "Mmm Hmm. I was just trying to get to know the person who my granddaughter will be spending so much time with."

But Mary couldn't shake the feeling that Lexi was bad news. Her intuition gnawed at her, leaving her uneasy.

Shortly after Mary's questioning, Layla and Marcus returned home from grocery shopping, greeted by Mary's presence.

"Hey, Mom," Layla and Marcus chimed in unison.

"I hope you weren't harassing the sitter," Layla joked, breaking the tension.

"Actually, she was," Lexi interjected, her annoyance evident.

"MOM!" Lexi's sharp tone sliced through the air.

"Well, I just had a few questions that y'all may have missed in the interview," Mary defended herself.

"Please don't run off the sitter," Layla pleaded, frustration coloring her words.

"I'm trying to run off your husband and the sitter," Mary muttered under her breath, her distrust lingering.

As Lexi concluded her shift and left in her little red sports car, Mary couldn't resist peeking out of the kitchen window to watch her drive away.

"It's just somethin' 'bout her. I can't shake this feeling," Mary murmured to herself, her intuition still unsettled.

Title 43: Unseen Eyes

A few weeks had past and Lexi finally gained the family's trust. As the evening descended upon Marcus and Layla's home, Lexi took a calculated risk. With Layla, Marcus, and Mary out of town for a church conference, the opportunity arose for Lexi to invite her boyfriend, Damion, over while she attended to Hannah. With Hannah tucked safely in her bedroom, Lexi and Damion settled onto the couch, indulging in the luxury of relaxation.

Their laughter filled the air as they flipped through channels, the glow of the television casting shadows across the room. For a moment, they forgot the world outside, wrapped up in each other's company.

"Isn't this nice?" Lexi said, snuggling closer to Damion. "Just the two of us, no interruptions."

Damion nodded, a smirk playing on his lips. "Definitely. It's been too long since we've had a quiet night like this."

Lexi leaned in to kiss him, savoring the moment of closeness. But beneath her outward calm, her mind buzzed with worry. She stole glances at her phone, half expecting a message from Layla, but there was nothing.

Meanwhile, Layla, out of town, unaware of the impromptu visit, grappled with technical difficulties from afar. The monitoring system she relied on to keep an eye on her home was on the fritz, leaving her unable to check in remotely. It was an unexpected frustration, leaving her feeling disconnected from her daughter and the place she held dear.

Back at the house, Lexi and Damion reveled in the temporary freedom, blissfully unaware of Layla's struggles. They joked and teased, enjoying the rare opportunity to unwind together. But beneath the surface, Lexi couldn't shake a lingering sense of unease. Despite her best efforts to maintain a façade of normalcy, the weight of secrecy pressed upon her.

"You seem tense," Damion observed, his tone laced with a hint of suspicion. "Is everything okay?"

Lexi forced a smile. "Yeah, I'm fine. Just... thinking about stuff, you know?"

Damion's eyes narrowed slightly, but he didn't press further.

As the night wore on, they remained ensconced in their bubble of bliss, oblivious to the unseen eyes that would have watched over them, had Layla's monitoring system been operational. And as Layla's absence stretched into the night, the boundaries between trust and deceit blurred, leaving Lexi to grapple with the consequences of her actions. Unbeknownst to her, Damion's past held secrets far darker than she could have imagined.

Chapter 44: Unsettling Shadows

The night wore on, the gentle hum of the television providing a backdrop to Lexi and Damion's subdued conversation. But as the drinks flowed, their inhibitions loosened, and soon, Lexi succumbed to the comfortable embrace of sleep, her head resting peacefully against the arm of the couch.

In the dimly lit living room, the silence was shattered by the sound of footsteps. Hannah, roused from her slumber, emerged from her bedroom, her eyes wide with confusion as she laid eyes on Damion. Without hesitation, she retreated back into the safety of her room, a sense of unease settling in the pit of her stomach.

But Damion followed, his steps heavy with intent as he crossed the threshold into Hannah's sanctuary. He loomed over her, his presence casting a shadow over her innocence. "What you doing Retard?" he murmured, his words a twisted echo in the stillness of the night.

Hannah, with her limited grasp of sign language, struggled to convey her fear and discomfort to the intruder in her room. She signed frantically, her hands trembling with apprehension, but Damion remained oblivious to her silent pleas.

Instead, his gaze lingered on her form, his eyes betraying a hunger that sent shivers down Hannah's spine. She felt exposed under his scrutiny, her vulnerability laid bare before a stranger who showed no signs of empathy or understanding.

The sudden ring of Lexi's phone pierced the tension, jolting Damion out of his trance. With a swift movement, he retreated from Hannah's room, leaving her alone in the suffocating silence.

On the other end of the line, Layla's voice carried a hint of concern as she checked in on her daughter. "Shhh, be quiet!" Lexi hissed, her voice strained with urgency as she reassured Layla of Hannah's well-being, her words a desperate attempt to conceal the chaos that threatened to unravel within their midst.

Unbeknownst to Lexi, her boyfriend harbored a dark secret, a violent history that loomed like a shadow over their fragile existence. And as the night stretched on, the shadows deepened, casting doubt upon the safety of Hannah's sanctuary.
As Lexi watches Hannah retreat to her room with her dinner, a sense of unease settles over her. She tries to push aside the feeling, convincing herself that Hannah is just being her usual shy self around Damion. However, deep down, a voice whispers warnings that she's learned to ignore over time.

Meanwhile, Damion sits at the table, a charming smile playing on his lips as he reassures Lexi that he'll be leaving soon. But his mind is elsewhere, consumed with his own agenda. He surreptitiously slips a substance into Lexi's soda, a move calculated to ensure she falls into a deep sleep soon.

As Lexi finishes her meal, she notices Damion eyeing the house keys hanging from the rack in the kitchen. It's a common sight in the household, but tonight it sets off alarm bells in Lexi's mind. She knows she should confront him, demand to know his intentions, but her love for him clouds her judgment.

Eventually, exhaustion creeps in, amplified by the effects of the substance in her drink. Lexi bids Damion goodnight, barely able to keep her eyes open as she stumbles towards the guest bedroom.

Left alone in the dimly lit kitchen, Damion's true intentions come to the forefront. With a stealthy glance around to ensure he's not being watched, he pockets one of the spare keys from the rack. His plan is simple: wait until Lexi is sound asleep, then sneak into Hannah's room.

Hours pass, and Lexi succumbs to the drug's effects, slipping into a deep slumber. Unbeknownst to her, Damion moves quietly through the house, his footsteps barely audible as he makes his way towards Hannah's room.

Meanwhile, inside her sanctuary, Hannah senses a presence outside her locked door. Her heart races as fear takes hold once again. But when she hears the soft click of the lock, panic sets in, and she braces herself for whatever comes next.

Outside, Damion hesitates for a moment, the weight of his actions pressing heavily on him. But the desire for what lies beyond that locked door drives him forward. With a steady hand, he inserts several different keys into the lock, the mechanism finally giving way with a barely audible click.

As the door swings open, revealing the darkness within, Damion crosses the threshold, his intentions sinister and his resolve unshakeable as he begins to sexually assualt Hannah. And in that moment, the fragile web of trust and love that binds this family together begins to unravel, setting off a chain of events that will change their lives forever.

Chapter 45: Unraveling the Truth

The next morning, Lexi's alarm wakes her, but she has persistent pain in her head. Unaware that the headache is from being drugged by her boyfriend the night before, she stumbles into the bedroom to check on Hannah, who seems to be disturbed and holding her body in pain. Damion had left the house abruptly after going into Hannah's room.

Hannah says, "Hannah hurt" to Lexi but Lexi has no idea what is going on with Hannah and thinks she may has some normal monthly cramping. Lexi gives Hannah some prescribed medication then removes Hannah's clothing in order to clean her up before her family arrives. After removing Hannah's underwear Lexi notices that they are stained. Hannah again says, "Hannah hurt." After further removing Hannah's clothing she notices minor bruising on Hannah's body and then starts to panic.

"Oh shit. What happened?" Lexi is nervous because she can't recall some of the episodes the night before. She hurry and bathes Hannah and tries to come up with a lie for the bruises on Hannah. "I'll just say she stumbled after I mopped the floor. After dressing Hannah she calls Damion to see if he can fill in some of the pieces of his visit the night before but he does not answer her phone call. "Shit! Let me get myself together before they get here. calm down Lexi, calm down." she tells herself.

Lexi decides to give Hannah some pain medication. After a few minutes of taking the medication Hannah has calmed down, but the bruising will still have to be explained. Layla called to check on Hannah and to inform a nervous Lexi that they are will be home shortly. After the phone call Lexi goes back into the room to check on Hannah. After pulling back her covers, Lexi finds the spare key to Hannah's bedroom laying on Hannah's sheets. "Oh my God!" Oh my God!" Lexi screams out. Lexi looks at Hannah and bursts into tears as the revelation of what may have happened to Hannah unfolds.

Lexi again picks up the phone and nervously dials Damion, but still he does not answer. Lexi is hoping that Ms. Mary does not come home with Layla and Marcus because Ms. Mary is already suspicious of her. Layla and Marcus pulls up and hour later which gave Lexi time to get herself and her story together. Lexi distracted Hannah by putting on her favorite show. "Hey baby, we missed you!" the couple replied. Hannah remained focused on they toys and the show that she was watching. Marcus looks over at Layla..."Well, I guess she didn't miss us."

As Damion remains unreachable, Lexi's anxiety mounts. She can feel the weight of the situation pressing down on her shoulders as she tries to maintain a facade of normalcy in front of Layla and Marcus.

Lexi's heart races as she watches them interact with Hannah, desperately trying to keep her composure.

With her notes submitted and Layla distracted, Lexi seizes the opportunity to slip away. She hastily gathers her belongings, her mind racing with questions and fears about what might have happened to Hannah the night before.

Outside the house, Lexi takes a moment to collect herself before pulling out her phone. She tries Damion's number again, her fingers trembling as she presses the buttons. Still, there's no answer. Panic threatens to overwhelm her as she considers her next move.

Feeling a surge of determination, Lexi decides to head to Damion's place. She needs answers, and she knows she won't find them sitting idle. As she drives, her mind races with possibilities, each one more terrifying than the last.

When she arrives at Damion's apartment, she finds the door unlocked. Her heart sinks as she steps inside, the air heavy with uncertainty. She calls out his name, but there's no response. She searches every room, her anxiety mounting with each empty space.

Finally, she stumbles upon a clue—a note hastily scribbled on the kitchen counter. It's from Damion, explaining that he had to leave town unexpectedly for a family emergency. The timing couldn't be worse.

Feeling defeated, Lexi slumps against the wall, tears streaming down her face. She's left with more questions than answers, and the weight of responsibility bears down on her shoulders.

But amidst the despair, a glimmer of determination flickers to life within her. She may not have all the pieces of the puzzle yet, but she refuses to give up. With renewed resolve, she wipes away her tears and vows to uncover the truth, no matter the cost.

After pulling herself together, Lexi calls to inform Hannah's parents that she will be out of town for training for the next couple of weeks. This will give Lexi time to track down Damion and find out the truth.

Title 46: Concerns and Confrontations

As the days stretched on, Mary found herself immersed in the daily routine of caring for Hannah. With each passing hour, her concern deepened, a nagging sense of unease gnawing at her conscience. Mary couldn't shake the feeling that something was amiss.

With a practiced hand, Mary administered Hannah's medications, hoping to alleviate her discomfort. But even as Hannah watched her favorite shows and played with her toys, the spark of joy that usually lit up her granddaughter's eyes was noticeably absent.

Frowning with worry, Mary picked up the phone, her fingers trembling as she dialed Layla's number. The urgency in her voice betrayed her concern as she relayed Hannah's continued discomfort. But Layla's reassurances did little to quell the rising tide of unease that threatened to engulf her.

"I hope that winch hasn't done nothing to my granddaughter!" Mary's voice crackled with emotion, the weight of her suspicions hanging heavy in the air. But Layla's dismissal only served to fuel Mary's fears, her motherly instinct refusing to be silenced.

"Mom, just stop. I'm quite sure Hannah is fine. I don't need you flying off the handle," Layla's words stung with a sharpness that cut deep. But Mary refused to be deterred, her resolve hardened by the need to protect her precious granddaughter at all costs.

As the hours ticked by, Mary watched over Hannah with a vigilance born of love and concern. With each passing moment, the walls of denial crumbled, revealing the harsh truth that lay hidden beneath the surface. And though the road ahead was fraught with uncertainty, Mary vowed to stand by her granddaughter's side, a steadfast guardian against the darkness that threatened to engulf them all.

Layla felt her mom was overreacting while speaking with her on the phone, even though her mother's voice trembled with worry on the other end. Mary believed Something was wrong with Hannah, something beyond the usual challenges they faced.

After coming home from work Layla witnessed Hannah's condition first hand. "What's wrong with mommy's big girl?" Layla called the doctor's office to schedule an emergency visit for Hannah hoping she could get an appointment the same day. There were no openings so Layla took the appointment for the following morning.

When the day of the appointment finally arrived, Layla and Mary accompanied Hannah to the doctor's office, their hearts heavy with apprehension. Mary's words lingered in the air, casting a shadow of doubt over their usually bright outlook.

As they sat in the waiting room, surrounded by the sterile scent of antiseptic and the low hum of conversation, Layla couldn't shake the feeling of unease that gnawed at her insides. She held Hannah's hand tightly, silently praying for answers.

Finally, the doctor emerged, his expression grave as he ushered them into his office. With a heavy heart, Layla listened as he delivered the devastating news—Hannah's physical examination had revealed signs of sexual abuse.

Layla's world shattered in an instant as she struggled to comprehend the magnitude of the doctor's words. How could someone harm her precious daughter? Anger, fear, and grief warred within her as she fought to remain composed for Hannah's sake.

Mary's hand found hers daughters, her mom's touch a lifeline in the midst of the storm. Together, they listened as the doctor outlined their options, his voice a distant murmur as Layla's mind whirled with questions and fears.

Hannah had to be rushed to the emergency room where she would undergo further testing. The local authorities and child protection had to be notified. Layla felt as though she were drowning in a sea of uncertainty. But amidst the chaos, one thing remained clear—she would do whatever it took to protect her daughter, to ensure that Hannah received the love and care she deserved.

Layla knew that Hannah was only left in the care of her in-home care providor, Lexi. With a heavy heart, Layla vowed to find the truth, to uncover the darkness lurking beneath the surface. Layla called to tell Marcus that he needed to come home, but did not disclose the devastating news about their daughter. News that would alter their lives forever.

Chapter 47: Shattered Innocence

Mary stayed by Hannah's side at the hospital so that Layla could return home and await Marcus' arrival. Marcus trudged up the front steps of his home, his heart heavy with the weight of the news he was about to receive. He pushed open the door, greeted by the familiar warmth of his house, but today it felt cold and unwelcoming. Layla was waiting for him in the living room, her eyes red-rimmed and swollen with tears.

As Marcus entered, Layla rose from the sofa, her trembling hands clutching a tissue. "Marcus, there's something... something terrible that happened to Hannah," she whispered, her voice quivering with emotion.

Marcus froze, his heart pounding in his chest. He felt as if the world had stopped spinning, as if time itself had come to a standstill. "What... what happened?" he managed to choke out, dread pooling in the pit of his stomach.

Layla took a deep breath, steeling herself to deliver the devastating news. "Marcus, Hannah wasn't feeling well, so Mom and I took her to see her doctor. The doctor told us about his findings," she explained, her voice trembling with sorrow. Our daughter has been sexually assaulted."

Marcus felt his legs give out beneath him as he sank to the floor, his mind reeling with disbelief and anguish. "No... no, it can't be..." he muttered, his voice barely audible as he struggled to comprehend the nightmare unfolding before him.

Tears streamed down Layla's face as she knelt beside him, wrapping her arms around him in a gesture of comfort and support. "I'm so sorry, Marcus... I'm so sorry," she whispered, her words echoing the agony they both felt.

For what seemed like an eternity, they clung to each other, their grief merging into a shared sorrow that transcended words. In that moment, they were united in their pain, bound together by the love they felt for their daughter and the unbreakable bond of family.

But amidst the darkness, a flicker of determination ignited within Marcus's soul. He wiped away his tears, his jaw set with resolve. "We have to do something, Layla... we have to make them pay," he declared, his voice trembling with righteous fury.

Layla shook her head, her own anger simmering just beneath the surface. "We will, Marcus... but we have to let the police handle this. We can't take matters into our own hands," she insisted, her tone firm but tinged with desperation.

Reluctantly, Marcus nodded, knowing that she was right. They couldn't risk jeopardizing the investigation, not when justice for Hannah hung in the balance.

As they sat in silence, grappling with the enormity of what had happened, Marcus's mind raced with thoughts of vengeance and retribution. He would stop at nothing to find the monster who had stolen his daughter's innocence, to ensure that he faced the full force of the law for his unspeakable crimes.

Meanwhile, Hannah lay in her hospital bed, her small frame fragile and vulnerable against the sterile white sheets. Though she couldn't speak, her eyes held a silent strength that belied her innocence, a resilience that spoke of the indomitable spirit within her.

Outside the hospital room, detectives worked tirelessly to unravel the mystery of what had happened to Hannah, their determination unwavering in the face of such heinous acts. With the help of a neighbor's doorbell camera, they had a lead to pursue—a description of a man seen leaving the house on the night of the incident.

But as they combed through the evidence, their hearts heavy with sorrow, they knew that the road ahead would be fraught with challenges and obstacles. Yet they refused to be deterred, driven by a sense of duty and a steadfast commitment to bringing the perpetrator to justice.

And so, as the sun began to set on another day, Marcus and Layla clung to each other, drawing strength from the love that bound them together. In the darkness that threatened to consume them, they found a glimmer of hope—a beacon of light that guided them forward on their journey toward healing and redemption.

Chapter 48: A Family's Struggle for Answers

Marcus sat at the kitchen table, his brow furrowed in frustration as he scrolled through his phone, reading yet another news article about the lack of progress in finding Lexi.

"They still haven't found her," he muttered, tossing the phone aside with a sigh.

Layla joined him at the table, her expression weary but determined. "It's like she vanished into thin air."

"I don't understand how someone could just disappear like that," Marcus said, running a hand through his hair. "She must be hiding out somewhere."

"But where?" Layla's voice was laced with worry. "And why hasn't she reached out to anyone?"

"I don't know," Marcus admitted, feeling a knot of anxiety tighten in his chest. "But until they find her, I can't shake this feeling of unease."

Just then, the doorbell rang, and they exchanged a glance before rising from the table to answer it. Ms. Karen stood on the doorstep, her warm smile a welcome sight amidst the uncertainty.

"Ms. Karen, it's good to see you," Layla greeted her, stepping aside to let her in.

"It's good to see you both too," Ms. Karen replied, her eyes filled with empathy. "How's my Hannah doing?"

"She's making progress thanks to you," Marcus said, a hint of pride in his voice. "She's spoken a few more words since you were last here."

"That's wonderful to hear," Ms. Karen said, her smile widening. "I brought some new materials for our session today. I thought we could work on expanding her vocabulary even further."

As they settled into the living room, Hannah's laughter filled the air, a reminder of the resilience that shone brightly even in the darkest of times.

Later that evening, as they tucked Hannah into bed, Marcus couldn't shake the feeling of unease that lingered in the air.

"Do you think they'll ever find Lexi?" he asked Layla, his voice barely above a whisper.

Layla sighed, her gaze fixed on their sleeping daughter. "I don't know, Marcus. But I hope so. For Hannah's sake, if nothing else."

"I just want this nightmare to be over, and the people who hurt my baby brought to justice. Even if I have to take matters into my own hands." Marcus confessed, his heart heavy with the weight of uncertainty.

"We'll get through this together," Layla said, her voice steady and sure. "No matter what happens, we'll always be there for each other."

Marcus nodded, feeling a glimmer of hope amidst the darkness that threatened to engulf them. Together, they would weather the storm, their love for each other and for Hannah a guiding light in the darkest of nights.

As weeks passed with no sign of Lexi, Marcus and Layla found themselves consumed by worry and despair. The once vibrant household now echoed with the haunting silence of uncertainty. They clung to each other, their hearts heavy with the fear of the unknown.

In a cozy corner of the living room, Hannah sat with Ms. Karen, her small hands moving hesitantly as she practiced her speech and sign language. Marcus and Layla watched from a distance, their eyes filled with a mixture of pride and anguish.

"You're doing great, Hannah," Ms. Karen said, her voice gentle and encouraging. "Keep going."

Hannah nodded, determination shining in her eyes as she continued to practice. Each word and gesture brought her one step closer to finding her voice, her spirit unyielding despite the darkness that surrounded her.

Meanwhile, in the heart of the bustling city, Detective Jeter and Detective Williams sifted through mountains of evidence in their search for answers. The case had consumed them, their every waking moment dedicated to bringing Lexi home and finding justice for her and her family.

"We can't give up, Jeter," Williams said, his voice resolute. "We owe it to them to find the truth."

Jeter nodded in agreement, his expression grim. "I know, Williams. We'll keep pushing until we get answers."

Their determination was put to the test as they followed lead after lead, each one leading to dead ends and false hope. But they refused to falter, their resolve unwavering in the face of adversity.

Meanwhile, Marcus and Layla received a shocking revelation about Lexi's disappearance. It was revealed that Lexi, the in-home sitter, had unknowingly harbored a man at their home who had had sexually assaulted Hannah. Desperate for answers, Lexi had gone in search of her boyfriend, Damion, hoping he could shed light on the situation. However, unknown to Lexi, Damion had a dark past, one that she had been unaware of.

As the truth unraveled, Marcus and Layla's anguish deepened. The realization that their daughter had been harmed under their own roof filled them with guilt and sorrow. But amidst the darkness, they clung to the hope that Lexi would be found unharmed, her innocence preserved despite the horrors she had unwittingly been drawn into. And so, they prayed for her safe return, their love a beacon of hope in the face of despair.

Chapter 49: Pursuit of Justice

As the days dragged on with no sign of Lexi and Damion, the detectives worked tirelessly, their efforts fueled by the desperate need for answers. Then, finally, a breakthrough came. A fingerprint match in the database provided a face to the man they were searching for: Damion Fisher.

Detective Williams' voice crackled over the police radio, "We have a match. Damion's face is in the system. Put out a BOLO. We need to find him."

The news sent a ripple of anticipation through the precinct. The hunt was on, and the community rallied behind the effort. Flyers with Damion's face plastered on them appeared on every street corner, in every shop window. People poured out of their homes, determined to aid in the search.

Layla and Marcus stood at the center of it all, their hearts heavy with worry yet buoyed by the outpouring of love and support. They watched as friends and neighbors joined together, united in their determination to bring justice for Hannah and their family.

"It's overwhelming," Marcus said, his voice choked with emotion. "I never knew we had so many people who cared."

Layla nodded, tears shimmering in her eyes. "It just goes to show how much Hannah means to everyone. We'll find Lexi and Damion, and we'll make sure they pay for what they've done."

Their love for Hannah fueled their determination, giving them the strength to face the uncertainty that lay ahead. And as the search intensified, they clung to the hope that their efforts would lead to the safe return of Lexi and the apprehension of the dangerous criminal who had threatened their family.

Detective Williams stood in the dimly lit hospital room, staring at Lexi's unconscious form lying on the bed. Wires and tubes snaked from various machines, monitoring her fragile state. The news wasn't good. Lexi had been found in a terrible condition, barely clinging to life.

"How is she, Doctor?" Williams asked, turning to the attending physician.

The doctor shook his head solemnly. "She's in critical condition. We're doing everything we can, but... she's lost a lot of blood. It's touch and go."

Williams sighed heavily, his mind racing with questions. If only Lexi could wake up and tell them what had happened, it might lead them to Damion. But for now, they were at a dead end.

Meanwhile, outside the hospital, news of Lexi's discovery had spread like wildfire. Reporters clamored for information, eager to get the latest scoop on the high-profile case. Among the crowd, Marcus and his family stood huddled together, their faces etched with worry and fear.

Back at home, Layla paced back and forth, her hands clenched into fists. "We have to find Damion," she said, to herself. "We can't let that bastard get away with this." Layla held onto Hannah as she pray for justice for her and Lexi.

But as the hours ticked by, with still no sign of Damion, the tension continued to mount. Detectives scoured the wooded area where Lexi had been found, searching for any clues that might lead them to her assailant.

As the manhunt for Damion intensified, Marcus's extended family approached him privately, asking if he wanted to join them in hunting for Damion and taking matters into their own hands. Marcus listened to their proposal, but after much consideration, he shook his head.

"No," he said firmly. "I won't risk hurting Hannah's and Lexi's case. We need to let the authorities handle this. We can't afford to make any mistakes."

His family members nodded reluctantly, understanding the gravity of Marcus's decision. Together, they continued to support him as they waited anxiously for news of Damion's capture.

And as the small community held its breath, hoping and praying for a resolution to the nightmare that had engulfed them all, Marcus vowed to do whatever it took to bring justice to Hannah.

As the night pressed on, Detective Williams and his team worked tirelessly to bring Damion to justice. Every lead, every tip, was followed up with unwavering determination. And then, a breakthrough came in the form of a call to 911.

"A suspicious individual matching Damion's description spotted at an abandoned house on the outskirts of town," the dispatcher relayed to Reynolds.

Without hesitation, Williams and his team sprang into action. They knew they had to move fast before Damion slipped away yet again. Racing to the scene, their hearts pounded with anticipation and adrenaline.

Arriving at the dilapidated structure, the detectives approached cautiously, their guns drawn but their voices firm as they called out for Damion to surrender. But there was no response, only an eerie silence that hung heavy in the night air.

Realizing they couldn't afford to wait any longer, Reynolds gave the signal for the tactical unit to move in. Clad in heavy gear, the officers advanced methodically, their senses heightened as they navigated the dark corridors of the abandoned house.

Tension crackled in the air as they moved deeper into the building, each step bringing them closer to their target. And then, suddenly, a sound—a rustle, a footstep—echoed through the stillness, sending a jolt of adrenaline coursing through their veins.

With precision and skill honed through years of training, the tactical unit closed in on Damion's location, cornering him in a dimly lit room at the back of the house. There, amidst the debris and decay, stood the man they had been hunting—a shadowy figure, his face twisted with defiance and desperation.

"Damion, it's over," Williams called out, his voice firm but tinged with the weight of all the suffering Damion had caused. "You're surrounded. There's nowhere left to run."

But Damion remained silent, his gaze flickering from one officer to the next, his mind undoubtedly racing as he assessed his options. Yet despite the darkness that cloaked him, there was nowhere left for him to hide.

With a swift and coordinated effort, the officers moved in, apprehending Damion without incident. He offered no resistance, his eyes hollow and vacant as he was led away in handcuffs, the weight of his crimes finally catching up to him.

And as the dawn broke over the horizon, casting its first light upon the town, justice had been served—for Hannah, for Lexi, and for all those whose lives had been forever altered by Damion's reign of terror.

Chapter 50: The Hunt Is Over

Meanwhile, back at Marcus and Layla's house, the phone rang, shattering the tense silence that had settled over them. Marcus answered, his voice strained with emotion as he listened to the voice on the other end.

"They've got him," Marcus said, his voice barely above a whisper. "They've caught Damion."

Layla let out a choked sob of relief, her hands shaking as she clung to Marcus for support. Their family, pastor, and friends gathered around them, offering words of comfort and support as they processed the news.

Later that evening, two detectives arrived at their doorstep, their expressions solemn as they briefed Marcus and Layla on the next steps. They explained that they would need to bring Hannah to the station to possibly identify Damion.

Marcus and Layla exchanged a worried glance, their hearts heavy with apprehension. They knew it wouldn't be easy for Hannah to face the man who had caused her so much harm.

"We'll take her in the morning," Marcus said firmly, his jaw set with determination. "We'll do whatever it takes to get justice for her and Lexi."

As Pastor Joseph arrived for prayer, they gathered in a circle, bowing their heads in solemn reverence as he offered words of strength and courage.

The next morning, Marcus drove slowly to the station, his mind racing with a thousand thoughts. Layla sat in the backseat, her hands tightly gripping Hannah's as they approached their destination.

As they pulled into the parking lot, both Marcus and Layla were overcome with emotion, their hearts heavy with the weight of what lay ahead. But they knew that they had to be strong for Hannah, to face whatever challenges lay in store as they sought justice for their beloved daughter and her caretaker.

As they entered the station, Marcus felt a knot tightening in his stomach. The weight of the moment bore down on him like an unbearable burden. Layla's hand trembled in his as they guided Hannah towards the designated waiting area.

Detective Williams approached them with a sympathetic smile. "I'll take you to the room where you can sit and wait," he said softly, understanding the sensitivity of the situation.

Relieved to be away from the bustling activity of the main area, Marcus and Layla settled into the chairs, Hannah between them. They held onto her tightly, their hearts racing with anticipation and dread.

Just as they were steeling themselves for what was to come, Ms. Karen rushed into the room, breathless from her hurried arrival. "I'm so sorry I'm late," she panted, her eyes filled with concern. "I'm here now. How is everyone holding up?"

Layla managed a weak smile, grateful for Ms. Karen's presence. "We're just trying to stay strong for Hannah," she replied, her voice quivering with emotion.

As the moment of truth approached, Detective Williams returned, ushering in the suspects. Each one stood with a large number above their head, their last names in their hands. The tension in the room was palpable as Marcus and Layla braced themselves for what was to come.

Hannah's eyes darted nervously from one suspect to the next, her breathing quickening with each passing moment. And then, as Damion stepped into view, her entire body tensed, a gasp escaping her lips.

Layla's heart shattered as she watched Hannah's reaction. She tightened her grip on her daughter, silently praying for strength to get through this ordeal. Marcus's jaw clenched with anger at the sight of the man who had caused so much pain to their family.

But amidst the chaos of emotions, there was a glimmer of hope. For in that moment, they knew that justice was within reach, and they would do whatever it took to ensure that Hannah and Lexi received the closure they deserved.

As Hannah's eyes fell upon Damion, her fear escalated, and memories of the harm he had inflicted upon her flooded back. She trembled uncontrollably, her small frame shuddering with each passing second.

Marcus and Layla exchanged worried glances, their hearts breaking at the sight of their daughter's distress. But they knew they had to stay strong for her. Karen stepped forward, her voice gentle yet firm as she spoke to Hannah.

"You're safe, Hannah. We're all here with you," Karen said, her eyes locking with Hannah's, offering a beacon of reassurance amidst the storm of emotions. "You can do this. Look at the men and show us which one hurt you."

With Karen's encouragement, Hannah's trembling hands slowly rose, her gaze shifting from one suspect to the next. And then, in a moment that seemed to defy all odds, Hannah began to sign. Each movement was deliberate, each letter formed with a determined effort.

"F... i... i... s... h... e... r," Hannah spoke softly, her voice barely above a whisper as she struggled to articulate each letter. But her determination was unwavering, and as she finished signing Damion's last name, a hush fell over the room.

Tears welled in Marcus and Layla's eyes as they watched their daughter's brave display. Karen's dedication to helping Hannah communicate had paid off in the most unexpected and crucial moment. And in that moment, they realized the magnitude of Hannah's strength and resilience.

As the suspects were led away, a sense of relief washed over the room. The family gathered together, holding onto each other tightly, finding solace in their unity amidst the turmoil.

"In the midst of trials, there was triumph," Marcus whispered, his voice filled with gratitude and awe as they embraced the miracle that had unfolded before them. And in that moment, they knew that together, they could overcome anything that lay ahead.

Chapter 51: A Legacy of Love: Building Hope and Empowerment

As they left the station, Marcus and Layla breathed a sigh of relief, grateful to be away from the prying eyes of the media. Hannah skipped ahead, her face radiant with joy, her hand clasped tightly in Karen's.

Back at home, the warm embrace of family and friends enveloped them, easing the weight of the day's events. Ms. Mary greeted them with a comforting smile, her presence a balm to their weary souls.

Hannah's eyes widened in delight as she entered the house, her smile widening at the sight of the spread laid out before her. Cake, ice cream, and all her favorite snacks adorned the counter, a celebration of her bravery and resilience.

But the true surprise awaited her in her room. Marcus and Layla had worked tirelessly to renovate it, transforming it into a sanctuary filled with sensory toys, a new bed, and dolls of all shapes and sizes. Hannah's face lit up with delight as she explored her new haven, her laughter filling the air.

As they settled into the warmth and comfort of home, Marcus and Layla watched Hannah's eyes sparkle with excitement and wonder. They exchanged a glance, silently affirming the love and determination that had brought them through the tumultuous events of the past days.

Ms. Mary, their pillar of support, moved gracefully among them, her presence a reminder of the enduring strength of family ties. She offered words of encouragement and affection, her wisdom grounding them in the midst of their joyous chaos.

With each passing moment, the love and gratitude in the room seemed to grow, a testament to the bonds that held them together. The foundation in Hannah's honor, a legacy born from her courage and resilience, stood as a beacon of hope for the future.

Inspired by Hannah's journey and the challenges she had overcome as a non-verbal individual with autism, Marcus and Layla knew they wanted to do more. They envisioned a foundation dedicated to providing support, resources, and advocacy for individuals with developmental disabilities, just like Hannah.

They shared their vision with their closest friends and family, who embraced the idea with enthusiasm and determination. Together, they began laying the groundwork for the foundation, reaching out to experts in the field, gathering community support, and raising funds to make their dream a reality.

Months passed, filled with hard work, dedication, and unwavering commitment. And finally, the day arrived when the foundation was officially launched, named in honor of Hannah and her remarkable journey.

The foundation's mission was clear: to empower individuals with developmental disabilities to reach their full potential, to advocate for their rights and inclusion in all aspects of society, and to provide support and resources to their families.

Through the foundation, Marcus, Layla, and Hannah's legacy lived on, touching the lives of countless individuals and families facing similar challenges. They knew that while their journey had been marked by hardships and obstacles, it had also been defined by love, strength, and the unwavering bond of family.

And as they stood together, united in their mission, they knew that their greatest victory of all was the difference they were making in the world, one life at a time.

About the Author

Shannon Williams is from the city of Alexandria, Louisiana, where she finds inspiration in the warmth of Southern hospitality and the rich tapestry of her community. With three children, seven Godchildren, and a precious granddaughter, Shannon's life is filled with the boundless love and laughter of family.

Writing has always been Shannon's refuge, a sanctuary where she can escape the shadows of depression and find solace in the power of words. Beyond her recently published story, Shannon is also a passionate poet, weaving emotions into verses that speak to the heart.

In her spare moments, Shannon can be found on her patio, surrounded by the soothing sounds of nature, as she decompresses from the challenges of the day and engages in heartfelt conversations with God. It's here, amidst the quiet whispers of the wind and the gentle rustle of leaves, that Shannon finds clarity and peace.

Driven by her love for family and a deep-seated desire to make a difference, Shannon is actively involved in her community, extending a helping hand to those in need. Whether it's lending a listening ear, offering support to local charities, or simply brightening someone's day with a smile, Shannon's compassion knows no bounds.

Through her writing and her actions, Shannon seeks to spread love, hope, and positivity to all those she encounters. With an unwavering belief in the resilience of the human spirit, Shannon continues to inspire others to find strength in their struggles and beauty in their journey.

Acknowledgments

I am deeply indebted to the individuals who have played pivotal roles in shaping my journey and supporting me along the way. To my elementary school teacher at Reed Ave. Elementary, whose unwavering belief in me ignited a spark of potential that I didn't recognize within myself at the time, thank you for your encouragement and guidance.

To my father, Charles Boss and beloved mother, Mary Williams, who's boundless love, sacrifices, and unwavering support have been the bedrock of my existence. Your belief in me has propelled me forward through every obstacle and triumph.

I extend heartfelt gratitude to my oldest daughter and biggest cheerleader, Karissa Patrick-Jeter, and her husband Mustapha Jeter, for their unwavering encouragement and unwavering support. To my daughter Trinity Patrick, my son Destin Henderson, and my granddaughter Kira Elize Jeter, your presence in my life brings immeasurable joy and inspiration.

To my extended family—the Williams, Boss, Conday and Jackson Family—your collective love and support have been a source of strength and comfort throughout my journey.

Special thanks to my sister Danita Adams, whose unwavering support and presence, despite the miles between us, remind me that I am never alone.

I am grateful to Pastor Joseph Franklin, his wife Sandra Franklin, and the Mount Triumph Baptist Church Family for their spiritual guidance and unwavering faith.

To all those who have stood by me, encouraged me, and never failed to support me in whatever I do, your belief in me fuels my determination and inspires me to reach for the stars.

With heartfelt appreciation,

Shannon Williams

64dcd90e-8676-4451-8f02-452286ca4dbbR01